Rosarium

YOUNG *Writers* CONTEST

The BookLogix Young Writers Collection

Attack at Cyberworld

Messages from the Breathless

Rapunzel: Retold

Nothing But Your Memories

Thieves of the Flame

The Girl I Never Met

The Silver Key

The History Makers

Embers of Empire

The Buried Laboratory

Into the Fire

Rosarium

Ambrea Richardson

BOOKLOGIX®
Alpharetta, Georgia

ISBN: 978-1-6653-0977-6 - Paperback
eISBN: 978-1-6653-0978-3 - eBook

Library of Congress Control Number: 2024948612

Printed in the United States of America

♾ This paper meets the requirements of ANSI/NISO Z39.48-1992 (Permanence of Paper)

1 0 2 5 2 4

It's an awful truth that suffering can deepen us; give a greater luster to our colors, a richer resonance to our words.

—ANNE RICE

CONTENTS

CONTENTS

CHAPTER ONE

Calm

Leo jolted awake as his head slowly slid down the cold car window, the lure of sleep tempting his body to rest. The early sky seemed frozen in time, and it wept angry tears that exploded against the car windows, beckoning to be let in from the morning air that encompassed all of the cars speeding toward their destinations on the eternally stretching highway.

Leo allowed his eyes to close again, a curtain dividing reality and an alternate plane of existence in which only he was present; an indescribable world that consisted of only thought and noise—a barrier, a refuge. His tense muscles were finally able to relax. His shoulders lowered from their tight position, his brow unfurrowed, his jaw unclenched. Even his thoughts were no longer racing.

These thoughts, tiny pulses of energy, stopped emerging to him as intensely as they had been hours ago. These pulses, if they were physical objects, would be small flares—ignited, thrust up into the starry night air, but with no purpose, warning against something unbeknownst to anyone. The intense anxiety and worry created by those little nightmares would cease, for now.

Leo allowed himself to exhale deeply and rested his head on his suitcase which sat beside him.

He no longer wanted to recall the horrors of having to participate in activities that others considered to be "fun," or relaxing even. He scratched faintly at the red sunburnt patch on his wrist as he recalled blackberry picking during his recent stay upstate with some of his parents' friends. The scalding hot sun that day had seemed enraged, especially toward him.

He ignored the pain as best he could because he knew the holiday was over, which had always been his favorite part of holidays. He felt isolated and alone, though surrounded by people, but they weren't there, at least not to him. An impenetrable barrier existed, a barrier which made him incapable of forming words eligible to ascend from the back of his throat. The vacancy existed, but was not physically present, as he could only sense it; his words, if he were to release them, would fall to the ground—unnoticed, meaningless.

There was no point; no one to talk to, no obligatory connection to anyone. He felt as though he were a caged animal who was let out on occasion to be fed, or to engage in unsolicited small-talk, like, "What grade are you in?" "How old are you?" "I haven't seen you since you were yay-high!" and the like. The older he became, the more he realized that it was as if those people were *required* to say such things to younger people, but he never really wondered why. He reluctantly went along with the act by simply providing the answers—answers which he was sure he had given at least a billion times.

Leo did have a great fondness for trips, however, especially long ones, but only the part that involved being in the car. He loved the feeling of waking up in the middle of those car rides: the intense, yet passive, feeling of not being in control and not having to worry about it, and being able to have a brilliant, simple excuse for doing absolutely nothing. It was strange for him to fathom that riding in a car seemed productive because you're going somewhere, but as a passenger you aren't contributing, yet somehow it feels as though you are. And your reward for being the non-contributing passenger is to enjoy peering out the windows and feeling no responsibility, no worry—a summary of what Leo wanted this summer to be, just like the perfect real-life scenarios he had contained within his mind.

His eyes were pried open once more when the weathered station wagon began rattling as his father drove too close to the edge of the highway and spit curses under his breath. The heavy atmosphere of the cold, enclosed space intensified as the loud, crunching gravel crackled against the tires of the car.

Leo tensed up, raising his shoulders, the rocks beneath them a non-terminating ominous lullaby diluted by the sound of the loud rain. He assumed that they were still quite far from home; he couldn't seem to recognize any of his surroundings. The hushed voices of his parents were the ocean, coming in waves, lapping at the shore of his world in between sleep and consciousness. As the gentle rattling of the car windows lulled his brain into liquid nothing, the humming of the car, the white noise of the radio, and the occasional distorted voice emerging from the static of it all, beckoned him to sleep once more.

Every noise began to fade, one by one, as sleep took him. His eyes were weights, unable to be lifted by his fight to stay awake anymore. He gave in, and he gave in gladly. He drifted in, further, further, until he was no longer aware of anything anymore.

When Leo opened his eyes again, the car was pulling into the wide driveway of their house, the tall manor looming over him, frowning down at him from high above, each of its windows shining eyes.

The rain didn't seem to be letting up; it continued to come down in thick, slanted sheets. The house was crying, its melancholic aura coaxed out by the rain coating it with a soulless luster. His parents began climbing out of the car, while he lingered for a few moments longer, observing the altered, weeping landscape of his neighborhood that he had yearned to see for days. Now that he was home, the familiar yet still strange feeling of relief engulfed him, which always made itself present when he returned home after a long while. However, this immense disquiet, this fear that was always instilled deep within him, was not dissolved by the small assuagement of being home that was created. The calm, which existed just mere moments ago, was lost in the sound of the wind commanding the leaves on the trees surrounding the cul-de-sac to dance.

Leo's head whirled as the colors of dread and angst clouded his vision and tightened his chest. He swallowed hard. His heart raced. Beads of sweat began to form across his brow. Hearing the echoic drone of his parents' voices—which seemed to be coming from miles away—filled Leo with a sense of panic as he began to realize, as he got older, that he was truly alone. For seventeen years—alone in his short existence. However, for not much longer, he hoped, for soon he would be free to do or not do what he wanted. He hoped to leave and be far from home, so far that what he now called home would be a distant, unforgiving memory.

The small town of Thornbrook had a certain haze around

the townsfolk and shops that no one could seem to comprehend, but the enigma brought about immense joy and well-being—the feeling of life, the feeling of being a part of something. The trees swayed with the signs of the pastel shops and shiny people, always busy, always on the move, yet somehow always remaining the same; their eyes glazed over, their smiles lifeless, almost forced. The people like hollow shells, the buildings like ominous vessels.

As he sat, gripping his luggage, he began to quietly recall the times when he felt real, truly alive; discovering something new, thinking, creating, and realizing that he could never share anything with anyone, but he wasn't sure why. Another wall, another fortress, which seemed to keep him away from everyone he knew wasn't real, everyone he knew wouldn't understand him, everyone he knew who would stare at him with empty, lifeless eyes speaking in murmurs.

Leo was shaken from his panicked stupor when he heard the front door slam. He blinked rapidly and reached down to grab his other suitcase. After a great deal of struggling, he opened the door to the car, only to be immediately drenched by the downpour. His parents had already made it inside; it was as though they were never even there to begin with.

With a burst of sudden frustration, Leo kicked his oversized suitcase out of the brown leather seat, the creases and indentations laced with tiny stars of water. It hit the wet concrete of the driveway and burst open. He sighed and bent over to quickly pick up the spilled contents, eager to be inside—away from the chilly night air and pouring rain. He wiped the wet hair stuck to his forehead away, then dragged his mangled suitcase up the steep steps to the tall glass double doors of the house.

Everything seemed different, yet somehow the same. Everything was in place, the same way it was the day they had left, but all the dust had settled. All the life seemed to be drained out of the living room; an open space of nothingness, but an open space filled with many things. Nothing seemed familiar, even though he had seen these things all his life. The dining room, usually full of light and air—empty. The shag carpet, which stopped at the archway that led into the kitchen and out of the living room, was too perfect, the bulbs in the lamps too dull, the bright red fabric of the couch and old oval-shaped ottoman that matched the couch too dingy. A sour taste settled in his mouth as his mother removed the needle from the dusty vinyl record left on the record player, blew on it, and then allowed it to play again. Despite the somewhat disquieting feeling of being back home, Leo decided to appreciate where he *wasn't*.

But now he was back, away from the car rides, away from the cigarette-flavored air, from the constant drone that encompassed his brain in a serene crackling abyss. He hoped with all his heart that that was the last trip. He didn't know how much more he could take of the suffocating feeling of being miles and miles away from everything that was familiar, from everything that made him feel safe. The words of his parents' friends were meaningless, unsettling even—he couldn't comprehend why such things needed to be said.

For hours they would sit mindlessly in the garden and talk about what seemed to be absolutely nothing, yet the crisp, monotonous words that drooled down from their stiff lips seemed so vulgar and violent—sinister. Simple conversation about the merest of things was overshadowed by what seemed to be violent intent and insincerity. The seemingly arranged set of phrases that constantly circulated around them for days made him feel ill, producing a relentless sense of irritability he couldn't shake and cramps at the corners of his mouth, his smile being held up by an anxious puppeteer's strings.

Since he was barely acknowledged, he had no choice but to listen in on their chitchat. He sat for hours in that smoke-filled parlor, longing for freedom, longing to be anywhere but there. He sat silently, not daring to shatter the atmosphere of false merriment and sin. He sat, his thoughts swimming as the uneasy feeling of his usual paranoia gained on him, leading him to believe his internal monologue was being heard, loud and clear, by everyone; every word, every criticism, every detail. This perturbed, indescribable feeling stuck strongly with him, even now. Even in this moment, fading phantoms of the all-too-familiar experience made themselves more and more at home inside of him. He could still see their glazed-over, unnaturally aware eyes following him, observing him, cutting like daggers into him; his tired eyes weak from pretending to have a connection to these mystery figures he had known all his life, but had not ever really known at all.

The fear is gone; nothing to worry about, he told himself many times, but his attempts to self-soothe proved fruitless as his heartbeat raced faster and faster, until he felt like he was going to burst. He curled his hands into shaking, sweaty fists, and proceeded to hastily walk through the living room, and up the spiral staircase to his room at the end of the hall, the cold air of the house biting him all over, making him shiver slightly.

He made it to his room, shutting the door quietly, and grabbed his raincoat from the side of the bed, throwing it on, buttoning all the buttons and flipping on the hood. He was supposed to be in bed, but he needed to calm his thoughts first, and he only knew of one way to do so.

He crept slowly to the window that overlooked the flooded neighborhood, the boisterous sound of rolling thunder shaking the glass. He unhooked the rusted latch and lifted the window-sill quietly upward and slipped through. He rested one of his feet on the thin ledge and the other on the desk against the wall, next to the window. With shaking hands, he grasped for the window above him on the third floor and began to climb the wooden grooves of the large house.

He passed the window on the third floor easily, which generated a great deal of surprise; he had never done this in the rain and half expected himself to plummet ten feet downward, which was always his fear during this ritual task. He glimpsed the ground and slipped on the windowsill, nearly losing his footing entirely. He made it to the top of the last window and desperately hoisted himself up onto the flat roof of the house, the slippery shingles threatening to send him sliding back down. Grabbing the adjacent gutter, he was finally able to achieve a steady balance. He fastened his jacket tighter around him and situated himself on the slippery roof, the water droplets falling from the tip of his hood and into his lap rhythmically, keeping time with the sporadic lightning flashing across the sky.

Leo looked outward and into the hypnotic storm, squinting, amazed; time stood still in Thornbrook, but it was time that still seemed altered. He could still recognize his cul-de-sac world even if it was painted in black and being hit with piles of wind and water from all directions; the same yet different. The concrete circle was a paradise, a cradle of everything he loved, especially the river. It wasn't just any river, but one where, if he looked closely into its murky waters, he could see the memories that he held there.

Tomorrow was when the fun would begin. As for now, he longed for nothing more than sleep. His eyelids were heavy, his whole body yearning and beckoning for rest. The excitement for something so immensely insignificant and uneventful, however, was overwhelming. Just the thought of finally being home and back with everything he recognized filled him with a rejoicing, ecstatic feeling that made his spine tingle and his heartbeat dance.

As a goodbye to his stay on the beloved rooftop, he reached into the gutter and pulled out the assortments of rocks and sticks that were lodged inside, throwing them up into the air. He wiped his hands on his jacket and made his journey back down, stealthily climbing down the windowsills until he reached his room.

He cracked the window open a little bit more, and tumbled inside, his head hitting the wall by the small bed—hard. Flustered, Leo tossed his jacket into a corner by his suitcase and threw himself onto the bed without bothering to close the window, the rain sprinkling the small wooden desk with fat, clear droplets.

He slept heavily that night, comfort and satisfaction engulfing his thoughts. Leo's wet hair clung to his head, the water forming a soggy halo over his head and onto the soft fabric on which he rested.

CHAPTER TWO
Stranger

Leo awoke with his ears ringing, the usual silence of the house especially overwhelming him this morning. He would have to grow used to it once more. He got up, running his fingers through his matted hair, his stomach churning with excitement as he thought about how great today would be. The more he avoided thinking about what he wanted to do today, the more excited he got. Maybe, he thought, he would go pay Willie a visit.

His jovial feelings were building, knowing his parents would be leaving for work soon, which meant he would have the spacious house all to himself. The rain was beginning to ease. The sun was emerging from its resting place. He walked over to close the window he had foolishly left open all night and used his hand to wipe the water from his cherrywood desk. He stuck his head out the window, closed his eyes, and inhaled deeply. Warm, nature-scented memories rushed back to him, and he felt as if summer daisies filled his lungs.

He looked around his room with new eyes, seeing every object in his presence in a new light. It felt as though he had been standing still in that exact spot nearly a lifetime ago. He was back after what seemed like a lifetime of enduring endless interrogations about his life, a perpetual game of choosing the right answer and fighting the urge to walk away in the middle of the small-talk. It didn't feel like it, but it had only been a couple weeks. His seashell collection, his overly stuffed bookshelf, his posters—a sense of belonging came over him to his satisfaction, a feeling he had not experienced in a long while. Not bothering to change clothes, he made his way downstairs, running down the steep stairs eagerly, skipping steps.

He was enticed by the smell of coffee and the sweet yet potent smell of the vanilla candle that stood proudly on top of the stone mantle. It was morning, and he couldn't wait until his parents were finally, *finally* gone. With his mind alive with ideas, he tread lightly into the parlor to find his parents sitting stone-faced in the spacious room, each in their own world. Their faces were neither emotionless nor expressive, but rather somewhere in between.

His mother, Mary Kaylock, had just gotten up to turn the record she had been playing over, placing the needle delicately, jumping a little at the sudden sight of Leo when she turned around again. Except for the warm sound of a gentle piano sonata that played from the slowly spinning record, there was an otherwise eerie silence lingering, hanging heavy in the air. This was how it always was. Leo was used to it. Out of fear of what would become of his mind if he thought too hard about why things were the way they were, he never questioned it. Ever. Although they seldom spoke to each other, Leo always felt as though he had a strong connection and bond with his parents. They said so little, and reacted so little, almost as if they didn't exist at all, which on most occasions he greatly appreciated.

This time of day was the only time Leo would usually get to see them. He didn't really mind, as he preferred to be alone and always found others—besides himself and Willie—odd. He wished it wasn't that way, but he had always, by no fault of his own, described himself as an irritably anxious person who liked quiet hobbies. However, once his parents *did* leave, he always found he wasn't particularly fond of the big house by himself, accompanied only by the stairs creaking and the occasional cold drafts drifting down the deserted hallways, whispering to him that he was alone. The air that filled the interior of the house felt like plastic, every breath hot and arid. This contrasted deeply with the outside air. When he opened the door there was moist, dampening dew that clung to his lungs and fog that choked his vision. The fog surrounded what was still visible of the cul-de-sac in what appeared to be clusters of dainty white sylphs.

The clinking of forks against china led Leo back to his parents, his mother, now clad in a blood-red shawl, hunched over her coffee, creating small galaxies as she stirred her spoon in the steaming void.

"Good morning, Leo," his mother whispered, her eyes barely meeting his intent gaze. Her grip on the smooth ceramic mug tightened. Though her small, calloused hands looked wicked, she, in fact, wasn't. Leo could always tell when his mother was there, but not with him, when the spaces behind her diamond eyes were vacant houses.

He sat down slowly beside her, attempting to follow her gaze, confused. He could never understand why she always looked so melancholy and distraught, her once-radiant smile that had shown like the sun itself had been quieted, never to be revealed again, covered by the moon. He had begun to notice her—and everyone else's—cumulative decline around the time of his tenth birthday. It was now seven full years later, and nothing had changed, but Leo tried to ignore this fact, for his sake. It made him worry if it was something he had done, but he could never think of anything, so now he found himself simply shrugging it off and trying to break the barrier she put up between them by making conversation. He should be allowed this much, he believed.

Chester, Leo's father, didn't have to say a word. For brief moments, his stare was a warm embrace, a soft field of clover. But there were certain moments where it was cold and distant, as if someone else was inside, showing himself at sporadic moments and then flickering away again. Chester was an open man—vacant, yet all-revealing eyes providing the manuscript of all his thoughts, not a single thing was hidden.

The three sat at the intricately fashioned wooden table in the middle of the large room, the table creaking gently with every stir. Chester looked on elsewhere, his wire-framed glasses glinting in the orange, newly born sunlight pouring into the quiet room. His gaze into nothingness made Leo somewhat uncomfortable, but he tried to ignore it.

Leo glanced out of the full-length window across from him, spotting the river near the adjacent houses. He longed to run his fingers through the cold rushing water, the contact smooth and gentle, engulfing his fingers in a gentle caress. He was too excited to eat anything, the outdoors beckoning to him. He took one final fleeting look at his obelisks for parents, slid his shoes on without bothering to tie them, and began his day. As soon as he opened the stained-glass door, a slight breeze rushed into the dimly lit house, creating a subtle, pleasant chill that ruffled Leo's hair, leaving it in scattered brown layers atop his head.

First, he wanted to find Willie. They did everything together, even if it meant doing nothing at all, and they had done this for as long as either of them could remember. Leo eagerly ran through the dense undergrowth behind the end of the large neighborhood, the forest surrounding him in deafening silence. He walked over to the clearing that the two frequented nearly every day during the summer, which contained a deep river of crystal blue running through the patches of greenery that made up the lush overgrown grass and bush that grew wild by the banks of the river.

He sat down on a large rock, carved and marked on nearly every side; a physical representation of their entire history at this river—a sacred visualization of a friendship that consisted of mostly useless activities. Leo really hoped that Willie might be around here. He dreaded the thought of having to knock on his door, because there was always the chance that Mr. Laurent, Willie's father, would arrive at the door before Willie did. It wasn't that he had anything against the enigma of the man; it was just that he was a very strange person to be around. He was a man of very few words, his tall stature making his silhouette a crooked phantom, looming over everyone, his poor hygiene evident. His clothes were rarely ever different from one day to the next, and he reeked of a putrid smell that never seemed to leave him. His eyes were glazed over with fog, his matching mind elsewhere.

Leo let himself slide down, his back against a tree, his feet inches away from the meekly flowing water. He snapped a twig off one of the branches hanging precariously over his head and began to stir the rippling waves of the water around with it. He decided he would wait around here a little longer before he considered going to Willie's house to fetch him. Leo, however, didn't want to waste the whole day waiting around, because it was already getting tediously boring, rapidly.

Since Leo seldom came to this area alone, he quickly realized there wasn't much to look at. He had experienced it

11

all before and had noticed every facet of every rock, every imperfection on every tree, and every divot in the ground. He watched a clustered town of tadpoles mixed with frog eggs float through the tender waters that held life so dearly in its compassionate liquid hands. He knew that he could count on Willie to arrive soon because this was something they always did—always. It wouldn't be long before Willie would run up and be right next to him, he hoped.

A few moments later, Leo heard light footsteps rushing across the soft fields of grass and pine needles. Leo looked up from drawing anxious lines in the dirt with his finger, swirling it around in the water a few times to clean it off. He then turned around and was met with Willie's signature wide grin, his thick, long curls flying behind his back as he ran toward Leo. Willie's mischievous and boyish appearance along with his occasionally spontaneous personality made him appear to be significantly younger than he was at times. He reminded Leo of a dirty buccaneer.

"Hi, Leo!" Willie yelled, tripping several times before sliding down next to Leo atop a nearby slippery rutted rock. Leo rolled up his jeans and stuck his feet in the water, creating small ripples in the warm flowing waters. The two sat in silence for a while, skipping stones across the crystal stream. Willie shattered the silence, turning his head to look at his friend.

"So, what's happening? How's it feel to be back in Thornbrook?"

"Great. They were all so . . . weird."

"How come?"

"I don't know, it just felt . . . off, like I was doing something wrong." Leo sighed, picking up a rock and throwing it to the side.

Willie turned his attention back to the river, twirling his fingers around in a circle, making tornadoes in the water. He looked at Leo and smiled faintly. "Well, I'm just glad you're back. I had nothing to do except be stuck in my dad's stupid library all day. I read so. Many. Books. It was terrible."

Leo looked at him. "As often as you talk about hating books so much, I'm starting to think that you actually love them." He smirked.

"What? No way, quit talking that nonsense."

Leo shoved him into the water and laughed. Willie's head emerged from the clear water, his eyes squinted as he pushed his long locks out of his face, revealing his wide, nearly ever-present grin, his teeth further accented by his tan skin, glowing golden in the morning sun. He grabbed onto the bank and climbed back on the rock, dripping water from above onto Leo.

"Hey! Watch it," Leo exclaimed as the cold drops made their way down the back of his shirt. He glanced up at Willie, only to be splashed by his dripping hands.

Their conversation wilted, leaving a comfortable silence again that engulfed them for quite a while. Leo felt something brush across his foot and looked down, lifting his leg, creating wavelets that spread throughout the width of the river. Willie followed his gaze, confused. Upon looking closer, he cracked a grin.

"Wait, no way! Hang on, be still," he said. He bent over and scooped something out of the murky water.

Leo glanced into Willie's cupped hands. He looked up at Willie and shrugged. "So what, man? It's just a frog."

Willie's eyes went wide. "*Just* a frog? Look at it. It's so . . . cool looking."

Leo averted his gaze and chuckled. "Yeah, okay."

"Remember when I snuck up on you and poured all those frogs I caught down your shirt and you screamed? That was gold."

Leo's embarrassment from that moment returned, as he felt his face and the tips of his ears slowly growing hot. He sighed and laughed. "Come on, gimme a break. That was years ago, and to be fair, I didn't hear you coming. At all."

Gently, Willie allowed the small, slimy creature to squirm into the water with a small slapping sound, which echoed in the thick silence of the woods.

Suddenly, Leo felt the hair on the back of his neck stand on end. His spine tingled, and a chill ran through his body. He felt as if he was being watched—closely, intently, carefully. He whipped around, squinting through his overgrown, unkempt bangs to see beyond the clearing and into the rest of the dense woodland area. He caught a glimpse of someone, like an apparition, their shadow gone almost instantly. Then he laid eyes upon the small figure, the movement appearing to dance through the thick shadows that lay beyond the two in the distance.

He turned back to Willie, who looked puzzled by Leo's unexpected paranoia. Leo stood up abruptly, quickly removing his feet from the water, slender legs soaking wet. He swallowed hard, his head filling with fear.

"Hello?" he called out into the woods, whose thick undergrowth seemed to swallow up his already hushed voice entirely. He heard rustling—twigs snapping, leaves crunching. Confused, Willie glanced around the clearing to try to figure out what Leo was hearing.

When Leo looked again, the figure he had seen moments before—a mere shadow gliding along with the many other shadows created by the golden sun—had moved closer to them, becoming clearer and clearer. At this moment, Leo was able to get a closer look at the mysterious figure—a girl.

She emerged reluctantly, pulling herself slowly out of the shadows, her hands pressed nervously against her sides, which made her seem smaller than she already was. Her hair, the color of night, covered most of the sides of her face, its luster giving the midnight tresses a multichromatic appearance in the light of the midday sun filtering through the trees. She was a nymph in the eyes of the two boys—a tiny, scared fawn caught in headlights in the middle of a desolate road.

CHAPTER THREE

Day

The dancing shadows from the trees looming above cast dark stripes across her face, contrasting with her pale lips and eyes, blending into the dark ringlets of her hair. Her silver eyes went wide when she noticed Leo had spotted her, and she ducked behind an adjacent bush that shielded most of her from them. She was trapped and frantically looked to her right and then to the left, her eyes darting back and forth, searching for a way to disappear, to seep into the ground, to dissolve.

Willie, shielding his eyes from the sun, got up and approached her slowly, radiating confidence, but with hints of hesitation—a rare contradiction as he usually found himself to be an assertive person. Each step he took, his excitement grew to a new level, yet he tried to remain slow.

Leo was sure that to the girl, Willie seemed anything but approachable. The look on her face made it seem like she wanted to run, to fly away, but found herself planted—no—*rooted* to the ground, her eyes wide with a pronounced fear.

Leo glanced over and looked into her dancing, shattered-glass-patterned eyes and saw her discomfort that practically screamed at them to leave her be, and he couldn't help but feel a pang of remorse. He knew Willie wanted to talk to this girl, and he had already decided that. He knew that even if he had decided that he felt uncomfortable with Willie approaching her, it was far too late—Willie was now right in front of her, looming over her. He smiled softly, the shadow of his spindly, tall figure shading her small, freckled face.

They were plants, deep contrasting plants—a tree casting a curtain of darkness over a timid wildflower, deprived of willingness by the tree's shade. She cowered like an autumn leaf in the brisk wind hanging on to its branch, her bright eyes searching for signs of danger, millions of thoughts in her head, painting millions of different possible outcomes to this encounter. She remained tense and unmoving, her jaw clenched so hard she appeared as though she might shatter her teeth. Her fists were balled up tightly and glued to her sides. Willie began talking.

"I'm Willie, that's Leo." Willie smiled wider. He pointed to Leo who lingered in the distance, still peering in their direction suspiciously, uncertain as to why Willie would want to talk to anyone else. Leo shot him an angered look, his eyes evident of intense contempt and resentment toward Willie's sociability . Willie, of course, paid no mind, and gave him an overly enthusiastic wave, continuing to maintain the mellow atmosphere that he always seemed to create wherever he went. Leo furrowed his eyebrows at Willie as the mysterious girl's gaze followed the direction of Willie's gesture, causing him to accidentally lock eyes with her for a fleeting moment before both of them simultaneously looked down.

"D'ya wanna be friends?" Willie jutted out his firm hand for her to shake. At this moment, Leo found himself increasingly uncomfortable, as he realized that *he* was now the one hiding himself away, not her, and he decided he refused to give off this kind of impression. With that, he waded through the shallow river water to get to them, his rolled-up jeans unraveling. He reached the other side of the bank, dripping wet, and positioned himself behind Willie, hoping to avoid any unwanted conversation with this enigmatic girl who appeared from what seemed like nowhere.

She stole glances at Willie through her thick hair, appearing to remain careful not to draw too much attention from either of them, but slowly allowed herself to relax, dropping her shoulders. There was a heavy silence that hung above their heads for a few seconds, and Leo felt as though the whole forest, every breath of life, every breeze, stopped to lean in and listen attentively to what she was going to say.

Her whole body seemed to shrink in size in the shadow of the two strangers as she parted her lips to speak. "I'm . . . Day," she said quietly, playing with her hair, and looked down abruptly, scraping at the dirt with her feet.

The hesitant, gentle wisp of her hushed voice was lost in the wind and was barely audible to Willie or Leo. The air around them seemed to suddenly grow more humid and dense before Willie spoke, cutting through the fog, with sunbeams exiting his mouth with every word. Leo's shoulders relaxed a little, and his jaw unclenched as Willie began to speak again.

"Oh . . . well, nice to meet you!" he exclaimed with genuine enthusiasm that made Leo seethe with rage . He wished meeting new people was this easy for him as it was for Willie.

The two watched as Day managed a faint grin at one corner of her mouth for a quick moment before returning to her numbed demeanor. She twirled a lock of hair between her fingers over and over seemingly waiting for something—anything—to happen.

Slowly, carefully, she relaxed every muscle in her body, a starved tiger emerging hesitantly from its prison, her overwhelming shyness that seemed to hold her back from everything slowly fading by the second.

The two boys studied Day, each of them withholding millions of questions, daring not to speak a word, careful not to scare her off. Leo took his place beside Willie, realizing this stranger seemed to be . . . nice.

"It's okay, we don't bite. Well, at least *I* don't," Willie said finally, gesturing toward Leo, hoping to get Day to laugh. The small girl merely smiled faintly and let out a sharp exhale—a sound that somewhat resembled a hushed laugh—before beginning to twirl her hair around her fingers once again.

Leo exchanged concerned glances with Willie as they both began to pick up on her anxious behavior, which took on characteristics of extremity that neither of them had witnessed before. Leo knew it had to be frightening Willie the most, because he was the one who approached her in the first place, and he knew he only wanted to help her—he knew he could. Despite the fact that Day, to them, appeared to be roughly the same age as he and Leo, she was nearly two heads shorter than Willie, who was tall for his age, and one head shorter than Leo.

Willie put his hands on his knees and bent down to her level, looking her in the eyes. Leo rolled his eyes, as he thought the gesture was a bit strange and insulting. She maintained eye contact long enough for Willie to realize that he was even being acknowledged by the girl at all. He spoke in a friendly, loud voice. "Hey, so I know you're pretty freaked out right now . . . I think, but do you wanna come hang out with us? Over there? We have our own spot by the river and everything. There's a whole lotta stuff to do, like sit on rocks, catch frogs, skip stones, have mud fights, and—"

"Okay," replied Day, a hint of eagerness in her voice.

Willie nearly jumped in surprise at her unexpected reaction that seemed out of character, even though he barely knew the girl and they had only met moments ago. Without a word, he began to lead her back to where they were lounging by the river, with Leo lagging far behind.

Leo still felt somewhat apprehensive about talking to Day. He felt an odd similarity to her, which caused an aversion he couldn't quite wrap his head around. He was trapped in a feud that only involved himself—a one-sided thought battle that threatened to tear him apart. Her hesitation, and shyness toward what seemed like anything and everything was echoic to his own actions, and an uncannily similar reflection of what he felt on the inside, a physical representation of all of his insecurities and fears, which made it uncomfortable to experience being around her. She reminded him . . . of himself. In order to discover what his unexplainable sudden abhorrence to this girl meant, he decided to just follow in Willie's footsteps and embrace and welcome her into their two-villager community.

With little regard to personal space, Willie sat next to Day on a cluster of rocks that were elevated several feet in the air. Day looked over to him, though she didn't move—her tensed shoulders and quiet demeanor clear giveaways to her discomfort. Leo positioned himself slightly behind the two, finding himself longing, yearning to find out what this "outsider" was all about. An uncomfortable silence lingered in the humid air for a few moments, before Willie looked down at Day, a grin creeping across his face.

"Hey, you should stick your feet in the water. It feels nice."

Day jumped at the sound of Willie's loud, booming voice, interrupting her uneventful internal monologue. Leo said nothing and looked into the rippling waters. Hesitantly, Day began to unlace her ragged, small boots, setting them aside carefully on a patch of moss that formed a slimy green cushion behind her. Slowly, she slid her feet into the calm rapids of the river. The murky water, a physical representation of all of their uncertainty about each other. Leo had finally begun to sense her uneasiness that understandably seemed to be directed at him specifically and decided that he'd have to talk to her eventually, so it might as well be now. He sighed. This was Willie's fault. He took a deep breath, mentally preparing himself, his nervousness stealing his voice. He cleared his throat, then hesitantly looked into her eyes and began to speak.

"So, uh, Day. We've never seen you here before. Did you move from somewhere else?"

Day looked up at him, her eyes filled with depth and intent. When she spoke, her voice was soft and quiet, yet forceful, and she spoke with a purpose, like the rain.

"No . . . I've been here for a while, actually. I'm around here a lot. I've never seen you guys before," she responded, brushing a thick lock of hair away from her face. Leo and Willie exchanged glances, perplexed.

"But we know everyone here. *Everyone*. If you were always around this river, and you've lived here for a while, we woulda—"

Day shrugged, her midnight curtains for hair bouncing, raised by her shoulders. Leo's embarrassment was masked by a short, fake laugh, cutting Willie off mid-sentence. Day looked at them both, confused, but somewhat content, glad even, to be included amid their banter. Throwing her long hair back behind her small, hunched shoulders, she pulled out a tiny, leather-bound notebook with ruffled pages and torn edges from one of the pockets in her floral-patterned dress.

Leo looked on with curiosity as the mysterious girl from the forest undid the single piece of twine holding the tiny book together and turned through the weathered pages, stopping at one page. The old, yellowed page was completely adorned with pressed flowers, of all varieties—rose petals, forget-me-nots, wildflowers, and even clover.

Leo watched intently as she floated over to a nearby bush of vibrant summer lilacs, her delicate pale skin like paper in the muted sunlight. With extreme tenderness, she began to gently pluck the small purple flowers, forcing them to abandon their stems. Day was a painting—so still and calm, but moving with

19

a guided reason and with dexterity and skill in such a simple task. She folded the flowers gently into her notebook, and then closed it as quickly as she had opened it, as if nothing had ever happened at all.

She looked up at Leo for a few moments and smiled as if she could read his thoughts, as if she knew how elegantly she could do even the smallest things. The rest of the afternoon, she walked along the banks of the river collecting flowers, the end of her dress soaking wet, creating a wet trail of dark dotted pathways in the dirt.

Leo and Willie said close to nothing the entire time. Willie tried to break the silence with small-talk but was uncertain of what to say. These quaint actions of hers, however, didn't stop Leo from having his doubts about whether or not she should belong with them. She was intruding. Or was she? He didn't know the answer.

"I've never noticed all these flowers here before," Willie said pleasantly.

Day smiled slightly. "Yeah, neither have I," she replied almost emotionlessly, gesturing down to the weathered notebook, filled with flowers identical to the ones she stood over.

Leo felt as though he had just been opened to a whole other world. He had never noticed the flowers. He never looked at anything—only the big picture. He was beginning to grow fond of what Day was teaching him. She was a teacher without even trying, showing him things about his own world, things he thought he knew. He was supposed to know everything.

Pretty soon, nightfall arrived. To Leo, it didn't seem like a gradual process, but rather a rush of darkness painting them black suddenly, the shadows running at them in waves, surprising them with no sun and a slight chill in the summer night air. Willie yawned obnoxiously, grabbed his shoes from the edge of the river and practically threw them back onto his feet.

"Let's go, it's getting kinda late," he said, climbing down from the highest rock, slipping, and nearly falling off the edge into the shallow water below him.

Leo nodded in agreement and followed him out of the forest and back into the paved cul-de-sac, with Day following close behind them, her freckled nose buried in her notebook, the pen she held in her delicate hand gliding along the weathered page rhythmically. This time, she wasn't pressing flowers, but writing something in rushed, tight letters that appeared angry in some way. Despite this, she showed no sign of being upset.

Suddenly, she stopped in front of a house neither Willie nor Leo had ever paid any significant amount of attention to until now, a house that seemed to arise from out of the mist, emerging from the dense undergrowth that seethed beyond it. To their surprise, and to hers, she smiled warmly, and looked up at both of them briefly.

"Well, good night," she said gingerly, walking off with a bounce in her step, one hand toying with her hair, the other holding her beloved notebook. As Day closed the large, black door behind her, she turned toward the boys, one last time, flashed a distant gaze that seemed to speak only to nonexistent spirits behind them, her small doe eyes filled with a prudence and an anxiety that neither of the two could pinpoint.

When she had made it inside, and was safely out of earshot, the two boys looked at each other, confused. Willie shook his head and laughed. "She makes no sense."

Leo shrugged.

Willie shrugged his shoulders as well, mockingly.

Leo rolled his eyes.

"Where did she even come from?" Leo said to what seemed like no one in particular.

"Who knows," Willie responded irritably as he scratched ferociously at his scalp covered by mountains of mousy hair and yawned. Leo squinted back at the house that seemed to emerge from nowhere. It looked out of place in the affluent neighborhood, mirroring Day herself. The flat, ranch-style, single-story home was seemingly drained of color, appearing to have been painted a fresh candy-floss pink before, but diluted, its original state lost in time. A windchime hung next to some potted ferns, which were placed awkwardly together on four spaced-apart rusty hooks. The white paint from the porch speckled the pale pinkness with a corrupting brown.

Day's eluding smile filled Leo with an insatiably strong urge to scream. His cheeks felt hot. He clenched his jaw in a poor attempt to relieve the intense burning that made his entire body ache with rage, yearning to push Willie away from the strange house and the strange girl that inhabited it, wishing she would appear outside again so that he could slam her own front door in her face. The longer he looked at it, the more he wished he could pick the entirety of the property up, hoist it onto his shoulders, and throw it as far away as possible. Nothing was going to get in the way of him feeling like he had at least one friend, and he knew he would do everything in his power to make certain of this.

As soon as he heard the door creak to a close, Leo spun on his heel and began walking back toward the clearing in the forest of which the two would frequent often this summer. *Two. Two. Two.* Leo repeated the word several times in his head. It sounded nice to him, and was how everything should be. Leo clenched his fists and his pace hastened with every thought of the girl. *Day.*

"Hey, Leo, wait up!" Willie shouted, panting as his brisk jog began to slow from a stroll to a walk and then what seemed to be barely a crawl. Despite his efforts, he was still several feet behind Leo. Willie puffed his chest and, with one last burst of energy, he ran up to Leo's heels, syncing his blissful strides with Leo's brooding, brisk shuffle.

Keeping his head to the pavement, Leo muttered to himself, and then to Willie, unknowingly maintaining a conscious distance between himself and his friend that acted as a sigil of protection for himself and his anger toward Willie.

"Why'd you take so *long?*" Leo said in a strangely familiar voice, almost whispering, almost yelling.

Avoiding contact with Leo's disdainful gaze, Willie picked apart the weathered parts of the sidewalk's concrete rocks with the tip of his shoe and shrugged, his eyes darting in every possible direction other than where Leo was standing, directly in front of him. Although Willie was much taller than him, Leo recognized that Willie still managed to find himself deeply afraid of him when he got into one of his "moods" as Willie liked to put it.

"Gosh, I don't know, man, I was just interested in making a new friend. It's always been us two. Don't you get . . . kinda bored? Why are you acting like this? It's . . . immature."

Willie didn't glance back up at Leo, keeping his head down as though his words were souring in his mouth.

Leo sighed deeply and turned slowly away from Willie, continuing the walk back to his house, his brisk, short strides were swallowed up by the darkening twilight wind, completely unheard on the normally echoic pavement.

Leo then broke into a run, unable to hear the slight sound of Willie's voice calling after him in the distance, his voice washed away by the crescendo of the wind weaving in and out through the surrounding dense undergrowth behind him, and as the rain began singing its ever-quickening song, Willie was lost forever in the thick haze that settled over the hot pavement.

Leo didn't care. He didn't care about anything, and he knew Willie didn't care about him. It didn't matter. He didn't need him anyway.

Leo hurried inside, so flustered he could barely think. He stormed through the living room, leaving wet, muddy footprints that created a path to the dining room, where he threw off his jacket and kicked his shoes off as he walked up the grand sloping staircase to his lonely, long, stretched-out wasteland of a corridor, which led to an empty, barren loft, which then led to the isolated tower that was his room.

He slammed open the door and collapsed on his bed, his wet hair clinging to the silk pillow that muted all sound that dared to attempt to enter his right ear. The sound of the rain intensified, as did the frigid chill that filled the air around him. A deep dark hole began to form in his thoughts that reminded him of the fact that he was now really, truly alone.

He cried hot tears that intertwined with the cold tears from the sky. Despite the constant chill that slid its dead fingers across his bones, Leo felt the strange warmth that was often accompanied by sorrow. As his room was illuminated by the blinding flash of lightning from outside his bedroom window, his mind began to clear. Willie had done nothing wrong—*he* had. Leo grew anxious as he began feeling as though he couldn't think anymore—too much sound, too many thoughts, too many people inside of his head, all with conflicting needs and wants, all against him, leaving him with no way to think.

Leo sat up on his bed as he was suddenly overwhelmed with the feeling that everything was his fault and that he was now hated by the one person he could trust, who he could talk to, who he could understand. This was the only thought that was clear to him in the brambles of what seemed like unfinished rationalities that he couldn't express in words, or even to himself.

Trembling, Leo held his breath until his lungs were on fire. He remembered his father teaching him to do this to calm down. He wasn't too sure exactly how it helped, but Leo was never hesitant to take his father's assertive advice, no matter how strange it could get. When the corners of his vision began to blacken and he began to feel increasingly light-headed, he exhaled slowly, which filled him with a deeply satisfying sense of warmth that flooded his insides and drastically slowed his formerly increasing heart rate that had caused him to break out in a cold sweat. Without realizing, he shut his eyes and slipped into a long sleep with a quality of which he had never experienced before.

Leo awoke to sunlight tickling his eyelids and the sound of rain dripping onto his windowsill from the slanted roof and the summer hymn of the birds and, worst of all, a headache that squeezed his temples tightly and caused them to pulsate with pain from even the slightest of movements. He winced as he stood up and the pain seemed to intensify as he once again caught a whiff of the pungent odor of coffee.

CHAPTER FOUR
Rage

Leo found that he couldn't stop thinking about Day, however, in the vague way in which he pondered the idea of her rather than what it would be like to be in her presence.

Mindlessly, he peeled off yesterday's damp clothes he had slept in and donned new ones.

He dashed hurriedly downstairs, pausing midway down. He could have sworn a faint weeping could be heard, prior to a loud crashing sound that rang out like a fairy bell, daintily quiet as though whatever had fallen had taken no effort to break.

Stumbling into the kitchen, he caught a glimpse of his mother cowering on the marble island in the center of her spacious sanctuary. But before he could part his lips to react, in the blink of his eye, in the raise of his eyebrow, she appeared to be sitting immediately upright in her usual reupholstered chair, staring blankly into the same coffee mug that never seemed to detach itself from her slender hands. The gentle big band music that droned jovially from the record player was stopped abruptly as his father, Chester, emerging from the shadows produced by the plum-purple curtains that tucked the light from the windows away, flicked the needle from the vinyl, aggressively removing the record to flip it over. After a few moments, a similar song began playing. Leo couldn't tell the difference.

After struggling to find his left shoe that he had so carelessly neglected to place with the right after throwing them in opposite directions the previous afternoon, he was reminded of his falling out with Willie. His heart sank and the familiar pit in his stomach had begun to form. He knew Willie wouldn't want to see him after all that he had said to him. He often would have seemingly invasive thoughts that questioned why and how he was able to be friends with Willie at all. Perhaps their equally strong personalities were too contrasting for each other, he often thought Willie, a loud, messy pirate, and Leo, his clever, questioning fox who trusted no one and feared many.

Leo's anxiety grew as he looked behind him toward Chester and Mary, whose lifeless crystal-ball eyes read back to him his growing uneasiness of being in the house with them. Despite the space being large and vast with plenty of room to do whatever he pleased, just the idea of their presence filled him with a feeling that he could not describe, not even for himself. However, he did know that the definition for this feeling would lie along the lines of emptiness, uncertainty, and most of all, a sense of feeling watched, trapped in a small terrarium in which he was being choked out slowly by the weeds and left to wither away into mere dust.

Their silences made him feel as though he were losing his mind, and the way they stared at him, watched him, and seemed to feed off of his terror and confusion—all of these things to him seemed to be becoming more and more frequent, and it drove him insane to not know what was causing such an odd thing. He often would wonder if it was something he had done, or if it had always been like this and he was just too aloof to know the true nature of the two people who were supposed to be the closest to him. *Two.*

Leo could recall, late one night, when he had crept downstairs to obtain a glass of water, he heard muted weeping coming from his mother, muffled by the wall that partitioned the parlor and the kitchen. Next to her sat his father, the voids in his eyes glossed over by the dimly lit chandelier that hung uncomfortably close to the dining table.

Leo had leaned in to listen better, squatting down close to the top of the stairwell, careful to remain completely silent. He remembered the jarring chill that traveled down his spine and formed gut-wrenching nausea in the pit of his stomach. He felt as though he were going to be sick as the cloudy air that surrounded them turned into a sickeningly hot moisture that made him feel faint. His vision blurred as his panic intensified.

Chester's eyes suddenly flashed rapidly back and forth as he had begun to chant. Black liquid oozed from beneath his eyelids. Mary cried louder. Leo then began to sweat, and his heart pounded hard in his throat as he remembered what it was like when he witnessed this—he vowed it to be the last time he would question anything, as he knew there would never be any closure, any explanation, no solace, which would keep him up for many days after. His way to cope was to find logical explanations.

But lately, this would not work. So, he thought, perhaps, that the brief visions were merely just dreams that had made their way into his reality, which was an experience he was somewhat familiar with. Leo spent many sleepless nights out on the roof or sitting on the windowsill that acted as a path out of his tower and made it a game to try not to fall asleep. These were the times everything would begin to change, from visions of vicious monsters to ravenous birds to the very speckled starry night sky caving in on itself. However, despite imagining these sights involving his parents to be dreams or imaginary, there was still the lurking truth that skulked in the back of his mind, which was the idea that the visions were of this realm, of reality, of his life.

His father cleared his throat loudly, returning Leo back to the present, back to immuration, back to purgatory, back to hell. He sighed deeply and cast his gaze toward the front door, which beckoned him to break free and go far, far away from here.

With his slight turn of the ornate doorknob, Leo gave in to its beckoning plea. Leo forcibly opened the door but not before he turned his head back to the dining room and spotted his jacket draped across a chair. Despite the summery warmth outside, Leo threw on his jacket, which he always wore. It provided him with a sense of protection, plus the surplus of sewn-in pockets always came in handy.

Leo ran out the door, his heavy running footsteps pounding hard on the sparkling cracked pavement, the blur of houses around him receding as he slowed, a carousel of spinning colors. He slowed his pace once he neared Willie's house, until he came to a complete stop directly in front of the large house that had a cunningly subtle arrogance to its weathered wood. The door was suddenly many, many miles away as his breath quickened and his heart beat so hard in his throat he felt as though he would be sick.

He trudged toward the door, dragging his feet as he went, creating a scratching sound on the weathered concrete that was nearly inaudible to him, unable to reach him through his anxiety. The first step seemed like an impossibly tall hurdle, or the spikes of a discontinued gauntlet. The windows and the columns and the door loomed over him, creating an ominously disturbed face which seemed to be perturbed by his intruding.

Everything fell silent as he made his way up the second stair. He stopped, then partially went up the third, but turned around to make sure the sudden tingly coldness he was feeling on the back of his neck was nothing, and not another unwarranted presence. The trees slouched down in the summer wind, as though leaning in to absorb his fear, swaying back and forth in a taunting manner, dripping their tears of hysterical laughter down on the world in the form of leaves, twigs, and debris.

The wind blew harder as Leo rang the doorbell, shaking. The raging storm in his head was calmed by the faint sound of Willie's dog barking that could be heard briefly before the wind tucked it away.

Leo waited. And waited. *No answer.* He shivered as the wind continued to blow and slowly backed up, careful not to trip backward on the steep steps.

Suddenly, the lock clicked and the door creaked open. Leo peered inside, trying his hardest to see past the darkness to focus on the silhouette that stood before him. He wasn't certain whether the figure was Willie's father, or Willie himself—they both shared the same figure and height, and the tall lanky build that seemed incapable of steadily balancing itself but somehow did. The figure stepped forward, birthing himself out of the darkness.

Leo's heart fluttered when Willie's father appeared in the doorway. He looked at Leo, but also managed to look beyond him, through him, to the empty roads behind him. He said nothing, and scratched at his long, dirty beard that covered the majority of the lower part of his face, his knotted hair caked and matted underneath a trucker's hat. Leo swallowed hard, clenching his fists.

"Is Willie here?"

Willie's father looked at him, his wide, unresponsive eyes

burning holes into Leo's retinas. With shaking hands, he raised a single finger, pointing to the right, gesturing toward the general direction of where their river was. At first, Leo wasn't certain of what the man meant, but he backed up and started walking through their backyard, making his way to the clearing.

"Thanks," he croaked, before quickening his pace, breaking into a run when he was sure Willie's father could no longer see him. Leo rushed through the clearing, sticks breaking loudly beneath his feet as he ran through the dirt, no clear path illustrated except for the way he knew in his mind, by heart. He spotted Willie sitting by the banks of the river, mumbling, quietly engaging in hushed conversation with what appeared to be himself. Willie jumped slightly as he heard Leo's bounding footsteps approaching.

"Jeez, Leo," he said, appearing to be somewhat agitated, but then let out a chuckle. Leo's nerves relaxed. He eased closer, brushing his fingers over the trees. He let out a deep sigh and began spilling out his apology.

"Look, I'm sorry. I didn't mean to overreact about her, I just—"

Leo's words were cut short as he took notice of the fact that there was someone else with them. Day sat calmly next to Willie, her hands folded delicately over one another on top of her sketchbook, which rested comfortably in her lap.

Leo's face fell as Day looked up at him, smirking, her cat eyes glistening with every movement of the trees that reflected off of the colorful orbs. Leo turned away quickly, ruminating in his angry embarrassment.

Willie groaned and pursued him, getting up and brushing the dirt from his pants. Day stood up as well, proceeding to take a couple of steps behind Willie before deciding to fall back to sit and wait uncomfortably at the corner of the slippery tall rock that faced the direction of Willie's chase. Willie's long, tall strides quickly caught up to Leo. In unison, the two looked back to make sure they were far enough away to where they would not be heard by Day. Leo glanced at her from the distance, watching as she nervously gripped inside the large pockets of her dress.

"What the hell is your problem, Leo?" Willie exclaimed

breathlessly. "You never give anything a chance. Why do you hate her so much? I just . . . don't understand it at all."

Leo looked down and shrugged, ashamed. Willie's eyes burned into the top of his head as he waited patiently for his answer. The silence hung heavy in the air as several more seconds passed. Leo couldn't bring himself to say a single word—he knew if he opened his mouth, he would say or do something he would immediately regret.

Leo unfurrowed his brow and unclenched his fists.

"Fine," he whispered through his teeth, doing everything in his power to restrain himself from punching Willie in the mouth. What frustrated him even further was not knowing why he was so angry, why he was so sad.

Leo noticed that when Day saw the two heading back toward her, she quickly put her head down, allowing her hair to drape over the side of her head that was visible to them, took out one of her charcoal pencils and—in an apparent effort to seem busy—began creating frantic lines that looked like nothing.

The three then exchanged awkward glances, trying their utmost to avoid eye contact with one another for too long, afraid of looking strange. Day kept her head facing firmly away from Leo. Leo had a strange feeling inside of him, an aching, elusive feeling that made him certain that he was doing something wrong. His mouth felt dry as he watched Day's shoulders stiffen, her arms locked against her sides, her fist wrapped so tightly around the pencil it appeared as though she might snap it clean in half. He knew what she was thinking. He knew it all too well, because this exact feeling had come over him countless times before, but this time it was different. This time, he was the villain. She was thinking he simply did not want to be around her, that there was a one-sided problem that could only be seen through his one-way mirror, on the outside looking in. She was thinking his natural demeanor was always apathetic and aloof, leading her to feel like an intruder. Leo's heart sank. He needed to mend this. Suddenly, her presence was like knives.

Leo forced himself to smile at her. It hurt the corners of his mouth, so he flashed it briefly before he began to walk away, standing closer to the edge of the river, hoping that one of them would say something. He hated initiating conversation, but he felt as though it must be done. He thought about it more and realized it didn't matter. As long as he could fool Willie into thinking they could all be friends, then nothing mattered to Leo. Nothing.

Playfully, he reached down into the river and grabbed a squishy glob of sand and mud and chucked it at Willie. He smiled impishly as Willie's face fell and Day gasped. With mud dripping down the side of his face, Willie abruptly reached into the water and grabbed a handful of mud and hurled it at Leo, laughing awkwardly, with undertones of uncertainty. Leo didn't say a word as he reached down once more, his hand marinated in the thick gloop. Willie stared hard at him. Leo knew he was trying to read his eyebrows and mouth, which intentionally left completely apathetic, remaining a blank canvas so that Willie would forget their feud and see that he was attempting to make an effort to have fun in Day's presence instead of remaining stiff. Within seconds, almost instantly, Leo realized he had made a mistake when he locked eyes with Willie and saw white hot rage, a burning frustration that had evidently been festering since the day before; now it seemed like Leo was doing this out of anger to embarrass him. To ruin everything.

Willie sprung up with a start, letting out a frustrated snarl as he lost control of himself, pouncing on Leo and hitting him as hard as he could as many times as he could, until he flailed around enough to the point where Willie's frail body was thrown to the ground, his head hitting the rocky surface, slippery with mud. He groaned in agonizing pain, gripping the back of his head with both hands, only to pull them away and see them covered in bright red blood that felt hot on his skin.

Both Leo and Day rushed over to him, their frantic voices reduced to faint echoing tones that were barely audible. Leo somehow managed to lift him up and drape him over his shoulders and carrying him unknown distances as he closed his eyes.

CHAPTER FIVE
Something Fun

Willie was tickled awake by the cold sweat dripping down his brow and the drool that coated his gaping mouth with a nauseating feeling. He glanced around—the room was almost completely black, save for a faint light coming from an adjacent room. The faint singing of a piano could be heard, as well as movement. The room smelled of old books and acrylic paint. Willie's heart began to quicken as he realized where he was—Leo's house. He sat up. Sure enough, Leo appeared in the illuminated doorframe, Day a silhouette behind him.

"I—are you okay?" Leo stammered. "You . . . took quite the tumble."

Willie squinted in pain as Leo turned the overhead light on. "Yeah. I'm fine," he responded shortly, avoiding looking up, afraid of his potential wrath.

"Here, drink this." Leo handed him a cup of green tea. "Careful, it's hot."

Willie grasped it desperately like a beggar with shaking hands.

"Thanks," he croaked, carefully setting the delicate china down next to him on the small decorative table.

His pain continued, if not intensified, with every sound he heard or every time he adjusted himself. He felt the back of his head—a thick bandage was wrapped around its circumference. He noticed the large quilt draped across his body, preventing him from moving much.

"We, uh . . . took care of you a little bit. I hope you don't mind." Leo flashed a smile faintly.

"Oh. Thanks." With shaking legs, Willie slowly unfolded and straightened out the blanket, positioning himself in between Leo and Day, who had both sat down. He allowed his long legs to sink slowly to the ground, sticking out from underneath the dense quilt. For what seemed like hours, the room was frozen in time. Unmoving, no conversation, only stillness. However, despite everything being so torn apart in the past couple of days, the heavy silence seemed to be stitching them together—strangers becoming acquainted by saying nothing.

Willie drifted in and out of consciousness as his eyes—windows that allowed him to periodically look around at the beautiful mess that was forming out of this day—closed heavily. Despite feeling guilty for everything that both he and Leo had done to each other, he thought it was glorious. Perhaps this was the beginning of the end of whatever had gotten into Leo. Perhaps this was the turning point and everything would gradually shift back to normal, with the inclusion of Day of course.

When Willie woke up again, he felt as though it had been at least an entire day. The study appeared to be exactly the same, albeit the fireplace was now lit, the flames making the shadows dance along the wooden walls, and Leo and Day were nowhere to be found.

Unmoving from his comfortable position, he allowed only his eyes to explore the large room that was filled with Leo's father's belongings, which ranged from vintage gumball machines to strange old toys to piles of phone books that seemed to stack all the way up to the ceiling, with ominously scribbled notes and photographs hanging out of the thin, yellowed pages. Chester was a strange man—Willie had always thought that. The mannerisms and actions of both Leo's parents—at least while in Willie's presence—reminded him far too much of his own father. It brought about an indescribable feeling that made him feel almost as empty as they must be.

As Willie began to drift in and out of being awake and asleep, he heard the door swing open loudly, the doorknob slamming into the thin wall, which was already significantly ruined in that one area, indicating it had been opened in this manner many, many times before. He jumped as Leo's heavy footsteps creaked across the wooden floor. Leo leaned down next to Willie, as Day cautiously looked on from the doorframe.

"Hey," Leo whispered quickly. "Do you wanna do something fun?"

Willie raised his head slightly, wincing as the increased

blood flow instantly filled his body with an overwhelming pain. "I—Leo, what time is it?" he responded weakly as he glanced over at the grandfather clock that loomed over their heads in the distance, the sound a beacon of life in a dead silent sea. It was three o'clock in the morning.

Willie groaned as he slowly slid off the couch, entangled in the heavy blanket that made him sink down to the floor quicker. Leo stared at his struggle before slowly offering him his hand, aggressively yanking him up.

Willie rubbed his eyes in agitation and attempted to comb through his untamable mane with his fingers, trying desperately to make it not stick out as much. He stared at Leo through tired, squinted eyes that felt swollen. His throbbing head begged him to sleep.

"I was thinking," Leo began, "we should all go to the attic." He smirked slyly in a manner of which Willie found troublesome to read.

Willie threw his head back in shock, opening his swollen eyes wide. "What are you talking about? Why? Your parents always told you that . . . that was the one place you should never, ever go."

Leo's smirk broke out into a grin, his teeth seeming to illuminate the dark room. "Well, guess what? I don't care anymore." He laughed, throwing up his arms wildly. "Let's go," he whispered, linking arms with Willie, dragging him out of the study and into the kitchen where Day now sat.

"Where even are your parents?" Willie stammered weakly.

"I . . . don't know. But whatever, let's hurry," he said, leaning him up against the island in the center of the spacious kitchen.

"Wh-why are you doing this now? You're *really* freaking me out."

Leo shrugged. "Why are you so confused?" Leo muttered, mimicking his tone. "You nag me all the time to explore the house, and now that I have this . . . weird urge to explore and now that I'm fed up with how my own parents are acting—with how most people around here are acting, and how everything feels in this shitty town—you're suddenly not interested." Leo sighed, then led them down the wide, long hallway.

Even though the ornate architecture that defined the house was evident, it was rather messy and unkempt—the elegant, patterned wallpaper was peeling in most areas and came off easily like the skin of an orange would. The house's walls were sprinkled with paintings of every size, their gold frames dull, lacking luster almost entirely. Leo felt a sense of pride when he saw Day and Willie look around in awe, although he wasn't sure why—he hated this place.

With sweaty palms and shaking hands, Leo pulled the short, braided string, unraveling the superannuated wooden ladder, splinters of wood jutting out of the broad sides. It creaked loudly before hitting the ground softly, the dust flooding the narrow hallway. He swallowed hard, his heart pounding in his throat—the only noise he could hear. He had thought of going into the attic once, not long before going on vacation. However, doing so made him quickly realize he absolutely couldn't, and so he descended immediately. He had felt a strong urge that beckoned him to climb up. But it was more of an urge, it was like an insatiable itch, as though there was something above him that he had forgotten, that he needed to know about.

He wasn't fond of tight spaces—the attic was like a hot wooden box, a furnace, with dust covering every inch. The small compact ceiling and walls inched closer and closer in on him every second he was in the parched garret.

When he reached the top, he sat down near the edge and looked down the gaping hole inches away from him. He dared not look around any further, unwilling to be acquainted with the surroundings of the old wooden coffin any longer than he had to. He looked up hesitantly as he heard Willie shakily make his way up the ladder.

Leo couldn't believe he managed to convince him to do this, nor that he had convinced *himself* to do this. Willie continued to climb the splinter-ridden ladder, its crying creaks ringing down the crimson-carpeted corridor. As he neared the top, Leo stood up slowly, his heart racing as he looked around. When Willie perched next to him with his legs dangling out of the small hole that was the entrance, a slight calm washed over Leo—he wasn't alone. Maybe this wasn't as bad as he thought. He relaxed his tensed shoulders. Besides, if Willie wanted them to do something fun all together, this was what he was getting—the ominous, unforgiving unknown.

CHAPTER SIX

The Attic

It was unbearably hot. Leo removed his jacket, tossing it aside. He smiled broadly at Day from above, almost grimacing, holding tight to the sides of the entrance with both hands. "Hey, are you coming or what?" he muttered snidely.

Day looked down bashfully, and stepped back, out of the way of the weathered ladder. "I think I'll stay down here. Actually, I should probably head home now. Everyone's probably wondering where I am." She stared down at the rough blood red carpet, awaiting a response from either of them.

"Oh, alright," Leo said quickly. "Do you . . . need us to walk you home or anything."

"No, I'll be fine," Day responded. With that, she walked down the hallway, disappearing as she turned the corner.

Leo tried to ignore his anxiety, his stoical demeanor convincing Willie he was eager to dig through old junk they had never seen. Leo was disappointed to find that it seemed there was nothing particularly interesting about the attic at first—just some old clothes, boxes, broken records, and several other miscellaneous items that looked as though they had definitely seen better days. However, driven by a sudden yet familiar madness that forced him to need to find out something, anything, Leo squatted down and began rummaging through a seemingly ancient, weathered cardboard box chock-full of various items and old pieces of paper.

Suddenly, Leo's face fell as he stopped fishing through the box, his eyes stopping on a photograph that stuck out from the rest. With shaking hands, he picked it up gently. "Check out this creepy picture."

Willie took the picture from Leo's trembling hands, horrified. The grainy photograph showed a group of people, all clad in deep-blue robes that covered their bodies entirely. This was topped off with grotesque masks, each one not like the other. The tallest person, on the far right, was wearing a mask that resembled a rabbit. Another was wearing a mask of a bear. The others ranged from cats, birds, and even a pig.

Their eyes weren't visible through the holes, instead appearing to be endless pits, like black holes. They were all clustered around what looked like a hanged man, with severely mutilated limbs, his grim expression forever burned into both of their minds. Willie turned the picture over. When he squinted, he could make out small, rounded letters on the back, written in messy, slanted handwriting. The words appeared to be a description of the photograph:

Thornbrook, Kaylock—1965

Leo peered over his shoulder to read the back. "That's weird. This was taken ten years ago. And *Kaylock* is your last name."

Leo broke out into a cold sweat, feeling increasingly light-headed. Any sense of calm he had felt just seconds before was completely lost in the swarms of dust motes that surrounded them. Everything seemed to blur together as he grabbed the photograph from Willie, flipping it over, and stared hard at the gruesome picture. His panicked concentration was broken by a soft snicker. Willie smiled and playfully nudged him.

"Chill out, it's probably just some weird coincidence, or a prank even."

Leo furrowed his brow and gave him a questioning sidelong glance. He knew Willie was messing with him out of spite for what he had done. He couldn't get mad.

Pretending to not be phased and trying his hardest not to let his fear propel his whole body to shake, Leo shrugged, setting the picture down on a nearby table, and redirected his gaze to a box of old paintings. The two remained silent for a while, both trying to think of anything else, other than what they had seen.

Willie found a box of old Edwardian-style hats and dresses. He laughed to himself as he slipped one of the silk dresses on over his clothes and sported a floppy, wide, feathered hat, complete with silk fabric flowers that hung daintily over the rim. He turned around to face Leo, unable to control his laughter.

Leo stared at him, confused.

"How do I look?" Willie asked, pursing his lips.

Leo shook his head and rolled his eyes. "Beautiful."

"Thanks."

Willie's impish manner and horrendously useless ability to jest in the most extremely unfunny situations only made Leo more tense. He realized he was alone as Willie continued to peruse through old creaky chests and discarded drawers, picking up a toy here, another shoe there, purposefully avoiding the ominous corner in which Leo had found the photograph . Leo continued to watch him in shock, his heart racing in his ears, making everything inaudible. He snapped.

"What are you doing?" Leo hissed. "Do you not realize—do you not realize what this means?" he exclaimed, holding up the weathered photograph. Willie immediately froze, and his impish smirk faded as quickly as it had formed.

"Sorry," he muttered weakly. "I just . . . don't wanna think about that picture. It's messed up. And I'm tired. Plus, it was your idea to come up here anyway, Leo."

Leo sighed. "Guess you're right. You should probably get going. It's late." He allowed Willie to feebly descend the ladder before making sure he was out of sight, then quickly slid the photograph off the dusty table. The glossiness of it stuck to his palm. He slowly slid it into his pocket, then headed back down, not speaking a word.

When Leo's feet hit the ground, he looked around on either side of the dark hallway illuminated by the pale moon that was beginning to fade. Willie was nowhere to be seen. All was silent, the thick carpet absorbing every cautious step he took. When he reached the kitchen, he thought he caught a moving glimpse of Willie in the window, or perhaps, someone else.

Leo laid in bed, holding the photograph above his head, taking in every detail, every tear, every blemish. Every time Leo closed his eyes, he could still see the mutilated man in the photo, his glazed eyes dilated in peril. After a while, he had stared at it for so long that the death in the photo meant little to him, but what did mean a lot to him now was *why*. His fear no longer came from the man's lifeless pleading eyes, or the robes, or the silly masks—it only came from the *why*.

CHAPTER SEVEN
All of My Roses

The next morning, Leo tried his absolute hardest to disregard the picture and focus on other things. He had fallen asleep with it on his chest. Peeling it off of his sweaty chest, he got dressed and climbed through the window, then slid down the roof and onto the dewy grass. He took a deep breath of the early morning air that tickled his nostrils and focused on his appreciation for feeling free. He closed his eyes as he walked, taking in the scent of the freshly manicured lawns drenched in a thin layer of water droplets. The hazy orange sunlight made everything feel artificial.

Leo looked up only to be met with Willie's gaze, his tired eyes like pits. Willie ran up to him in what seemed to be a rushed panic. He put his hands to his knees, gasping for air.

"Please," he wheezed. "I have something to . . . talk to you about." With that, Willie spun on his heel, leading Leo back toward the direction he was running from, and they walked slowly, saying nothing, until they reached Willie's house. He beckoned for Leo to come inside. The kitschy décor and the smell of books tickled his nostrils, filling him with an unidentifiable sense of belonging. Willie yawned loudly, shutting the glass door behind Leo.

The two walked into the quaint living room. Every wall was lined with a tall bookshelf, stuffed full of old books, piled up to the vaulted ceiling. The red leather couch groaned as the two sat down. The small, raffish house remained silent for a while. Leo allowed himself to relax, the gentle aesthetic of the small warm room absorbing him into the depths of unexplainable raw happiness. At the back of his mind, however, the image of the dead man's eyes still danced until he acknowledged them.

Willie broke the silence, rubbing his calloused hands together. "So . . . I was thinking a lot about that picture."

Leo clenched his jaw tensely at the mention of it. He felt relief that he wasn't the only one who couldn't seem to escape its influence. "What about it?" he started quickly.

"Well . . . I've been keeping something from you that I probably shouldn't have." He paused, tightening his sweaty hands into fists, glancing around nervously to make sure his father wasn't anywhere close by. "So, there's this . . . abandoned fabric warehouse—well, I'm pretty sure that's what it is—it has something to do with you." Before Leo could protest, Willie continued quickly. "And I know this because I've been in there a couple of times, and I've seen things that are a lot like that picture. Well, I'll show you." He sheepishly fished through the deep pockets in his baggy overalls and produced a small envelope. He handed it to Leo. In small, barely legible letters it read, *My garden is growing. It's working; all of my roses.*

Leo held it in his shaking hands as he traced over a signature that read *Kaylock* with a trembling finger. Sweat gathered between his eyebrows as Willie looked on over his shoulder, periodically stealing quick glances at Leo's reactions.

"Do you have anything else?" Leo asked slowly.

"No . . . that's all I have, and I've been holding onto it for a while. I didn't really wanna show you. I worry about that warehouse a lot. I'm not sure why."

Leo sprung up from the couch, making Willie's body jolt. "Let's go there. Please. I'm sick of having to try to get rid of my own curiosity. And if these things really *do* have something to do with me, then . . . I want to know. I *have* to." Leo followed Willie out the back door.

The walk was actually quite a long one, despite what Willie had said. Leo shoved his hands deep into his pockets and tried his best to keep up with Willie, who had broken out into a run. His feet pounded hard on the sparkling pavement in the summer heat. The march to the unfamiliar place was tense. The trees were new and brooding and the wind seemed to warn them against continuing their journey. Leo continued to follow close behind Willie's heels, careful not to stumble over any protruding tree roots that littered the ground like fallen soldiers on a long-forgotten gladiator battleground.

After what seemed like hours, the two finally reached a

heavily forested, seemingly abandoned, part of Thornbrook that Leo had never seen before. A large, squat building could be seen in the distance, almost completely covered in brush, with overgrown vines and greenery covering the boarded-shut windows and doors. There was broken glass everywhere, like diamond fractals embedded in the dry dirt.

Leo squinted and shielded his eyes from the neon midday sun and looked up at the ancient warehouse. A half-rotted wooden sign embedded in the dry dirt read:

KAYLOCK FABRIC WAREHOUSE

Willie followed his friend's gaze. "Weird, that's the third thing we've found with your last name." Willie raised his eyebrows, sighing, then walked toward a huddled mass of pine trees, rummaging through the plentiful needles until he found a sturdy stick. He aggressively pried off the flimsy wooden planks, which didn't take much effort. They fell to the ground hard. He wiped the excess small pieces of wood from his hands onto his pants, looking at the decaying double doors in triumph.

They both hesitantly stepped back, unwillingly absorbing the ominous atmosphere produced by the warehouse. It had several windows, all busted and cloudy. The small building looked to be screaming.

CHAPTER EIGHT

A Stack of Paper

Leo's breath caught like spiky briars in his throat as he reluctantly stepped inside, Willie close behind. The brisk summer breeze closed the heavy wooden doors abruptly behind them with a subtle whining sound.

Willie jumped. Leo was shaking. Every step they took brought about a wooden groan from beneath the floorboards.

The warehouse felt cold and still. Even the dust that was visible in the gentle sunlight projected through the windows appeared to be suspended in the air. The flat, wide warehouse reeked of decaying paper, and the smell of rotted wood and fabric tickled their nostrils.

The first floor was filled with old machinery and rolls of assorted fabrics, discolored from neglect and decay. The fabric was crammed into almost every corner of the open space, every fiber of it producing an awful indescribable odor.

Leo wandered down to a basement area, the stairs creaking with every uneager step. As Leo descended farther, he found himself more and more intrigued by this place. He yearned for closure, for any explanation of what was going on in that photograph. He felt drawn to this place, as if the answer would be here. He didn't want to be here—not at all. But he forced himself to carry on. It took all his strength to keep walking forward, to not turn back—to not run away.

Willie moved closer to Leo as the thin stairs began to take a spindling steep drop. Then Willie shattered the silence, his voice quivering. "We should've brought a flashlight, Leo. Let's get out of here. I changed my mind. This was a bad idea." With every word, his voice became more and more desperate.

Leo stopped a moment, shifting his weight, the wooden stair he was standing on swiveling a bit.

"Come on, don't you want to see what's down here? What

42

if there's a ghost?" he said, humoring his friend. Leo never believed in ghosts or anything of that nature.

Willie sighed. He walked ahead of Leo now, with quick long strides, his slender legs floating down the stairs.

Willie turned the rusted doorknob of what appeared to be an executive office. The intense odor of rotted paper and water damage hit them both at full force. The moldy office felt stuffy, trapping the two in almost unbearable discomfort. Water dripped rhythmically from the low ceiling onto the compact metal desk in the middle of the room.

The old desk was trashed with old documents, records, photos, and even newspaper clippings. Leo felt so tempted to look through these things, despite everything being covered in several layers of grime and filth. He couldn't stop himself from thinking about what might be revealed.

With shaking hands, Leo reached into the abhorrent stack, wincing as the mold tickled his palms and fingertips. His panic slowly numbed as he examined one of the intact newspaper clippings, skimming over it quickly, his eyes dreading to perhaps fall upon something terrible. He held the weathered paper in both hands as he brushed away the hardened dust on the singular stiff page, revealing an image of what appeared to be a house above the words that bled thick black ink. He tried to make sense of the murky print, but found the only legible words were "new addition," close to the very end of the paragraph. He furrowed his brow before setting it down on the opposite end of the desk. Willie looked on as he frantically picked up paper after paper, photo after photo, which consisted of images of what appeared to be the warehouse while it was in operation, various inventory notes, and a photo of . . . a house. He moved his thumb slightly to reveal a singular "F" in the corner of the last paragraph of the article, appearing to be freshly written in blue ink. He traced over the singular letter with his finger. Leo's heart raced in his throat as he felt as though he locked eyes with the house; its all-too-familiar gaping windows like soulless orbs. Although the grainy, black and white photograph left a lot of detail to be interpreted, he knew he was right; the tree that loomed over the front porch, the sloping hill right before the steep steps, the stretch of surrounding woods in the near distance—this was his house.

"No way," he croaked, his thumbs leaving dents in the fragile paper.

"What? What is it?" Willie replied hurriedly, turning his attention away from tracing his finger along the perimeter of the indented filing cabinet.

Leo practically shoved the paper in his face, exclaiming, "That's my house!"

Flustered, Willie snatched it from him, brushing the opposite hand on his pants in an attempt to remove the grime from it. He studied the photograph carefully, along with the two decipherable words before muttering dryly, "Yup. Looks a lot like your house." He looked at the photo a few moments longer. "That's definitely your house."

He looked up at Leo, whose eyes were practically vibrating with panic.

"A-and another thing; what the hell is 'F'? What does that mean?" he stammered, vigorously pointing at the corner of the paper.

Willie shook his head and shrugged intensely and slowly replied, "Um, 'Fun?' 'Freak?' *You're* acting like a freak, Leo, you have to calm down. It's just an 'F.' Is it hurting you?"

Leo took a deep breath, attempting to tame his racing heart that pounded in his ears before replying, "I just . . . want to understand something, anything. That's all. I can't take this anymore. This weird feeling I have about this town, lately. I can't shake it, and I feel like this could all be connected. So yes, it *is* hurting me."

Willie handed the paper back to Leo, who shoved it deep into his back pocket.

Leo looked down at his trembling hands, covered in a thick layer of slate gray dust that practically peeled away in one sheet when he briskly rubbed his palms together. He glanced back down at the desk that beckoned to him, littered with undiscovered material, the photographs and newspaper clippings screaming his name. *He needed more.* Tainting his freshly wiped hands, he dove them into the stack, sifting through what seemed to be receipts, documents of order histories along with photographs of the inventory. As he shifted the papers around in his hands to hold more, his heart sank as he began to find himself thinking that this was it. Suddenly, his hand stopped on something smooth, something that wasn't covered in a thick layer of dust. It felt *new*. He backed his hand out slowly, retrieving a barely intact manila folder. He reached inside, pulling out the entirety of the folder's contents. His fingernails were caked with the residue of old paper and mold.

From the folder, he fished out an even more intriguing photograph than what they had found in the attic. The photos were extremely similar, almost to the point where they could be identical, except for the horrific scene unfolding in the other. The people in this photo were the same as the last—clad in sagging robes and varying grotesque masks leaving them incognito.

The grainy black-and-white picture was extremely odd. The group seemed to be made up of about a dozen or so. They appeared to be all gathered around what looked like the river near the back of Willie's house.

Leo could feel Willie breathing hard over his shoulder and decided not to mention this to him. Unlike the attic photo, they all stood, looking ominously off into the fog as if all were a part of a machine in repose. Leo imagined if they were to emerge from the picture and come alive, they would all move and breathe as one. A stack of papers erratically fell out of the drawer of a busted filing cabinet adjacent to the small desk.

"I don't think we should be here anymore. It's uh . . . starting to get to me," Willie breathed, tugging gently on Leo's arm. Leo tried his hardest to look right into Willie's panicked green eyes, even though Willie was almost twice his height. Willie shifted his weight from foot to foot nervously, awaiting Leo's response.

"Five more minutes, I swear," Leo replied finally.

Willie glanced around nervously, his wild eyes like a jungle. "Okay," he responded, his voice quivering along with his body. He brushed off the wooden floor with the palm of his hand and sat in a corner, his arms folded tightly across his chest.

While Willie waited, Leo decided to explore further. He walked over to a dark, bare corner, with boxes piled high up to the ceiling, with immensely large amounts of black mold claiming most of them. He pulled one of the bottom boxes out, causing the entire stack to fall over, which hit the ground hard.

Leo jumped back, coughing, as spores floated through the air. His eyes watered as the dust was stirred about, causing him to sneeze several times. He left the toppled cardboard boxes alone, their contents too far damaged by water to be salvageable.

Shoving his hands deep into his pockets, Leo ventured upstairs for a bit, almost completely forgetting about Willie. He felt mesmerized by this place. He felt as though there was an invisible force yanking him, drawing him in deeper and deeper.

He ran his hands along the unused, rotted assortment of fabrics, looking for any kind of correlation between the warehouse and the photographs he had found. There was nothing there except abandoned equipment. This place was so normal; a place you would catch a fleeting glance of on a road trip and never pay any mind to. What were these photographs doing here? He reached into his back pocket and once again examined the tattered article with the photo of what appeared to be his house. He studied it hard, realizing more and more that there was no way he could deny that this was in fact his house.

Suddenly, he felt sick. He had to get out of here. He figured Willie would think he was taking too long anyway. As he walked back down the steep staircase to the basement, he could hear Willie's impatient stirring, accompanied by his passive-aggressive brooding that included overly exaggerated sighs and moans, which, even now, Leo found immensely amusing.

On their way out, Leo grabbed the folder and as many other things he thought would be significant and stuffed them all into the black holes he had for jacket pockets. He took anything that stood out to him—more photographs, newspapers, letters signed and addressed to people he didn't know, and that were dated years, decades ago. Anything that he thought might have to do with the people in the strange masks, he took. He would look at these later.

When Leo looked up, Willie was already close to the staircase, his eyes desperately searching for any sign on Leo's face that they were about to leave this forgotten place.

As they left the warehouse, Leo closed the door, hard. Willie breathed a sigh of relief, glad to be liberated from the stuffy, rotting building. The two ran down a poorly maintained backroad that carried them away from the woodlands.

Willie pointed excitedly to an area through the trees. "I thought we were lost, but the town center is just over there. How did people forget about these woods?" he said, moving his hand to push stray curly brown locks from out of his eyes. The sun shone down through the trees, casting abstract shadows onto the ground that added to the whimsical feel of the multicolored forest. The two jogged over to the paved clearing, becoming closer and closer to the familiarities of home.

The small town of Thornbrook had a certain haze around the townsfolk and shops that no one could seem to comprehend, but the enigma brought about immense joy and well-being—the feeling of life, the feeling of being a part of something. The trees swayed with the signs of the pastel shops and shiny people, always busy, always on the move, yet somehow always remaining the same; their eyes glazed over, their smiles lifeless, almost forced. The people, like hollow shells, the buildings like ominous vessels.

CHAPTER NINE

Somber Streets

L eo and Willie sat on a bench outside an old café they would often frequent during the school year, collecting their bearings. A man walked by, heading in the opposite direction of the majority of the people on the bustling street. Despite bumping into every other person, walking through them in what seemed like a stupor, he received no backlash. The buzzing people walked on, looking straight ahead, their eyes and minds possibly averted from consciousness. Leo stared at the uniform walk of everyone on the street. He wondered why it seemed like the only people who didn't look ahead blankly were he and Willie. Leo uncrossed his legs, glancing around uncomfortably. He nudged Willie on the arm.

"Did you see that?" he asked, a hint of panic apparent in his voice.

"See what?"

"Everyone was . . . walking so weird. That guy who walked by was just . . . bumping into everyone, and no one seemed to care."

Willie shrugged. "I don't know. Hasn't it always been like that? Quit thinking about things too much." Leo recognized Willie's tone, one he only used when he was trying to convince himself of something; he could tell Willie had noticed too, but was either lying to himself, or trying to keep Leo calm. Willie shoved his hands deeper into his pockets as chilly wind blew through the now quiet streets.

Willie's relaxed demeanor and tone of voice did little to relax Leo, or to make him think less about what he had just seen. If anything, it filled him with even more worry than before. He tried his hardest to just stop thinking about it altogether.

He loosened his grip on the withered papers inside his pockets. The breeze blew softly, ruffling his hair. Every time someone left the yellow-bricked café, the wind chimes atop the doorframe would sing and the mellow jukebox adjacent to the door could be heard.

The two sat there until the sun began to sink behind the bright assortment of buildings. The crowds of people, moving about like ants, began to thin out until just a few remained. The atmosphere changed, the air growing cold and dry as night had begun to approach.

Leo started to feel tense again. Willie spoke. "Remember last summer when we were swimming in that lake and . . ."

Leo couldn't hear anymore over his anxiety and rapid heartbeat that pounded loudly in his ears. He felt eyes burning into the back of his neck, through his hair, through his skull. He swallowed hard and dared to look behind him into the now-abandoned café.

He squinted through the colorful painted windows, his spine paralyzed by fear and uncertainty. Leo wasn't usually one to give in to fear—he always made himself face whatever he was petrified of, to show himself he wasn't weak.

But paranoia—that was different. It washed over him, drenching him in a cold sweat, a feeling of dread sinking to the pit of his stomach. He felt this feeling now, badly. His confidence was overcome by dread.

He didn't know what he was anxious about, but he knew there was something there. He couldn't take it anymore. He looked harder. He saw a faint, short silhouette. He felt the panic spread throughout his shaking, stiff body. Willie lowered his voice slightly and glanced at him, beginning to feel concerned. Willie's voice entered Leo's head in short fragments, bouncing off the closed windows of his mind, causing no interference. Leo's vision blurred. He couldn't think about anything else besides the apparition-like shadow that danced across the blue haze of his vision.

He dared himself to look back again, and there it was. Closer now—so close he could reach out and touch the cloaked figure.

Leo realized that this person was dressed in the same plain attire as the people in the photographs and documents he had been collecting. He could see the faint outline of two pointy

49

ears, clearly a part of the mask—this was the Rabbit. A quick chill ran down his spine as he continued to stare at the unmoving silhouette.

His blood ran cold, his mouth dry. Contrary to his constant calm nature he always tried so hard to maintain, Leo sprung up, nearly spilling all the contents of his pockets. Some things sprinkled to the ground, but he didn't care. He ran, with the only thing left in his mind—a now-shattered windowpane— was to get out. He never wanted to see the masked enigma again—ever.

Everything was a blur. All the shapes of the town he'd come to know so well were becoming a medley of black and white. His fear didn't allow him to concentrate on things that were practically meaningless at the moment, like color, sound, and such. He was getting away, and that's all he desired. The only sound that could be heard as Leo made a mad dash back to the clearing in the woods was the fast wind gushing through his ears, the cold air surrounding his head, encompassing him in a cold that cut like daggers.

He paid no attention to where he was running, nor did he care. Any place away from the Rabbit was where he wanted to be. His lungs were about to burst by the time he made it to the forest.

Panting, Leo allowed himself to sink slowly to the dry dirt, his tired legs weak. His vision faded in and out as he fell in and out of consciousness, out of reality.

CHAPTER TEN

Hot Chocolate in Summer

L eo awoke to Willie shaking his limp arm, his usual content expression warped by worry.

Leo's heart began to race again as he recalled what he saw. He sat up quickly, brushing the majority of the dirt off of his face and clothing. Willie furrowed his eyebrows.

"What was *that* all about? You just . . . took off running. What happened?" he asked Leo, more than likely perplexed by Leo's sudden outburst.

Leo looked up at his friend, confused. "How did you not see that? It—it was right there," he responded, his voice shaky.

Willie shook his head, his eyes wide in a wave of confusion. Leo couldn't concentrate. He couldn't look at Willie. He couldn't say a word or fill in the spaces of the sentences of what he wanted to say, the unfulfilled gaps in his mind like missing teeth.

Willie didn't question his friend any further for the complete silent duration of their walk home. When the two arrived in their familiar cul-de-sac, the aggressive red twilight marks that streaked through the cotton-candy sky matched the tense and uncertain atmosphere mingled with the satisfaction of making it home. They both sighed with relief, as it wasn't as late as they thought.

Willie and Leo jogged through the yards of grass for what felt like an eternity until they reached Leo's front lawn. Quickly, Leo removed the large amount of paper documents from his pockets and placed them on the ground away from his reach. He then began to unravel the adjacent garden hose from the wrought-iron post in the ground and squeezed the nozzle, letting cold, earthy water rid all of the caked-on dirt from his clothes and body.

Leo noticed Willie looking at him in disbelief. Willie knew Leo never liked to be drenched, and that he would never dream of becoming drenched voluntarily. Unsurprisingly, Leo knew he was thinking just.

"What are you staring at?" Leo smirked through the water, as he began to impishly spray him with the water, not stopping until he was just as soaked as Leo was .

Several hours later, the moon was out, providing a pale stage light for the thousands of pulsating fireflies. Leo and Willie sat on the porch shivering, waiting to dry off a bit before going inside, until Willie started to gripe about boredom.

Leaving their shoes on the outside welcome mat, the two eagerly sauntered into Leo's house. They realized how bitterly cold the humid summer night had turned. Leo lit the Victorian-style fireplace in the middle of the overly-decorated living room and prepared hot chocolate.

Willie didn't know it yet, but Leo decided that tonight was the night that he was going to get to the bottom of the pictures, all the letters, and all the intense anxiety and worry he kept bottled up from him, from everyone. He had decided he shouldn't bother telling his parents, for fear of what they would say, or if they would even believe him at all. However, he decided to open up to Willie and Day about it, as they had been there when he first discovered this perpetual web of mystery. He thought that now he would give Day an honest chance, and not just for Willie's sake. He was somewhat glad to know someone new and mysterious—an eternal anomaly of a girl.

Leo carried the two mugs of hot chocolate to the living room, careful not to trip. Willie took his cup and stared into the flames of the crackling fire, the steam rising from the mug mingling with the smoke drifting from the fire.

"So, what happened earlier?" Willie asked once more, removing his soaking jacket and draping it over a nearby loveseat. Leo sighed, removing his own jacket as well, taking his findings from the warehouse out of the pockets once more and spreading them all out across the wooden floor.

"Well," he began, "I saw this . . . person. They didn't . . . do anything. They just stood there, inching closer and closer. I panicked. Except, the thing was, he looked exactly like one of the people in the photographs, he was wearing a . . . rabbit mask," he explained, gesturing toward the first photograph of the masked figures they found in the attic.

"But why? That picture was taken ten years ago—1965, remember? Why would one of them be showing up now? That's stupid. Maybe you thought you saw one of them but it was just your mind playing tricks on you, you know? I can almost completely assure you that it was nothing."

Leo looked at the pictures, then back to Willie. "I can't believe you don't believe me," he exclaimed, massaging his temples, his heart pounding. "No, no. I'm completely sure I saw one of them—the one in the front with the rabbit mask. Its shadow was . . . following me; it was right behind us, Willie," he said, waving one of the weathered photographs in his face.

Willie shrugged before placing a supportive hand on Leo's shoulder, his wide eyes distorted with doubt.

"Would you do me a favor? I don't know *what* you think you saw, but can you forget about all of this, just for one day? Let's go camping tomorrow. I'll have Day come along too. Leo, for God's sake, it's summer—we're supposed to be having fun, not wandering around a creepy old building, full of who-knows-what, probably ghosts!" Willie laughed, instantly losing his seriousness as a grin crept across his glowing face. "I mean, I know it was my idea in the first place, but it turns out it was stupid. There's nothing interesting there. *At all.* We should forget about it."

Leo stifled a laugh; Willies over-dramatization of nearly anything and everything never failed to make him a little bit more calm, although the empty feeling of dread that had tightened its grasp on his brain nagged at his heart to beat fast and hard and for his shoulders to feel jittery and tight. "Okay." He shrugged from behind his mug of hot chocolate, taking a big sip and slightly burning his upper lip, which caused him to wince abruptly.

Willie looked over to his friend, rolling his eyes. Based on Leo's facial expression, he knew exactly what had happened. "You seriously couldn't wait until it was cool?" Leo forced a smile and shrugged. They both laughed, although Leo's was painfully forced.

****

Long after Willie left, Leo decided to disregard what his friend told him to do, at least for a while. He collected the dry, wrinkled papers from their place on the wooden floor in front of the dying fire.

Swallowing hard, he removed the thick contents of the manila folder, his wary hands hesitant. He pulled out a one-page letter, written in scribbled, spidery handwriting in thick black ink. It read:

Dec. 8, 1938
Dearest Floyd Kaylock,
 I regret to inform you that "act one" must be delayed; they're catching on, escaping. We cannot have this if we wish to succeed. Everything must be . . . perfect. Perhaps, years from now, with the deviants gone from Thornbrook, we will start again.
—N. Kaylock

Leo was afraid. What did it mean, act one?

He reached inside the folder again with shaking hands, desperate for answers, for closure. There were many other letters with greatly varying dates. It made no sense—1832, 1900, 1926, 1938. All of the other letters also mentioned something about performing an "act one " in Thornbrook.

Along with these letters were many other photos which also varied in date. However, instead of masked unknown enigmas in cloaks, the pictures featured close-ups of people. On the back, their names were written, all with the last name Kaylock, none of whom Leo recognized.

Leo's shock left him feeling cold as ice. He couldn't bear to look at any of it any longer. He ran to his room and threw all of the papers into his nightstand drawer, closing it quickly, as if to prevent the words of the mysterious letters from playing over and over in his head.

Suddenly, Leo felt exhausted, barely able to keep his burning eyes open. He collapsed onto his bed, not bothering to turn off the overhead light. He cleared his mind, thinking of nothing, concentrating solely on the black abyss behind his closed eyelids.

CHAPTER ELEVEN
Just Us

Leo woke up later than usual—it was almost twelve. He got dressed quickly, went downstairs, and prepared a single slice of toast, burning it. Sighing, he tore a piece off and ate it anyway.

Just as he took a swig of lukewarm tap water, there was a quick knock on the front door. Leo unlocked the heavy stain-glass door and opened it, revealing Willie, accompanied by a large duffel bag.

Willie smirked and raised his eyebrows. Leo's eyes went wide. "Oh yeah, camping, I forgot all about that."

Willie's face changed as he glanced to the side before looking down as he muttered in a hushed voice, "Oh, uh I should mention, my dad is coming."

"What? Why?" Leo said hurriedly, immediately disappointed in himself for showing his discontent.

Willie shrugged. "He was *really* persistent about going. He's stir crazy I guess, or something. I don't know."

"Alright," Leo breathed, before turning away to walk back upstairs. "Wait here."

Willie waited on the front porch for Leo to finish gathering his things from the spacious upstairs area. When he was done, the two jogged over to Willie's, where Willie's father, Mr. Everett, was finishing some last-minute packing of his own. Leo sat in the parlor, happy to be provided with orange juice and a warm blueberry muffin. He consumed it slowly, enjoying every moment of the sweet tingling sensation in his mouth.

Day appeared at the open front door, waving at the three warmly. Mr. Everett—perhaps a bit too eagerly—took her supplies along with everyone else's to the car, closing the trunk after placing everything inside. The three sunk into the leather-lined seats of the old car while Willie's dad smiled faintly at them through the clouded rearview mirror. His eyes seemed hollow, his smile lifeless. He tuned the nearly busted radio with careful hands, his slow-moving hands nimble—zombie-like—his raspy, nearly inaudible voice humming a forgotten tune.

Leo spoke up, despite his discomfort intensifying with every breath Mr. Everett took and every sneaky glance he flashed. "Hey, um, Mr. Everett? Thanks for taking us. Willie was telling me about how much you wanted to go."

The man looked at him for a split moment, his empty gaze meaning nothing, his eyes merely pits. Leo had begun to take notice of this nature and how his parents behaved similarly, creating minimal dialogue, seemingly not present—the resemblance was uncanny.

As they traveled on the streets that took them farther and farther away from town, there were less streetlights and signs, every unfamiliar tree looming above like a stranger. The car remained sickeningly quiet for most of the ride, tempting Leo to sleep.

****

When Leo awoke, he saw a small, empty parking lot, along with trees in all directions, as if enclosing the vibrating car completely in green. It was dark out. Everyone climbed out of the old car and simultaneously looked up. The parking lot of the campsite was on a rolling hill, bringing the group seemingly closer to the inky sky dusted with bright stars, no streetlights present to dilute their beauty.

Leo looked around, through the dense woodlands and the vast wasteland of a parking lot. Everything was quiet. Everything was still. "That's weird, we're the only people here."

Willie shrugged and proceeded to stretch his legs. With a sudden burst of energy, he began to assist his father in pitching the tent, with relative ease. Leo and Day were tasked with removing the group's belongings from the trunk. After she removed her share of the bags, Day stood idly by, patiently, her long black tresses lifted by the subtle wind. The crickets' chirping fell in and out of unison with one another, as if they were all engaging in intriguing conversation. Willie's father continued to pitch his tent, while the other three agreed on just sleeping outside, beneath the stars.

The deep hours of the night set in and left everyone awake

but Mr. Everett, who stirred quietly in his sleep every once in a while. Leo became increasingly paranoid about the abandoned campground. He found that a little more than a bit strange, but he chose not to say anything else about it, since he felt he was the only one who seemed to care at all.

The gentle night noises of twigs breaking in the distance and leaves rustling came from all directions. Despite the subtleties of these noises, it didn't feel like they were away from home at all. There were still sights and sounds all around, with everything busy, no matter the time of day. Leo felt at home here, amid the sounds, longing to experience, to touch, to lay eyes upon anything that moved—everything was a wonder, every corner of the trees in the forest a new, uncharted world. The smell of pine tickled his nostrils, beckoning him to explore the lush moonlight-drenched woods, with the full moon emitting clear, bright light.

Leo's blissful paradise was shattered by Willie's abrupt shouting bouncing off the branches of the trees in the forest that engulfed them almost entirely.

"Hey, Leo, will you come help me gather some wood?"

Leo nodded eagerly, yet somehow, he still felt his stomach tie itself in knots when he thought of venturing into the forest. He was filled with excitement, but fear still ate away at the back of his mind, constantly reminding him of what could happen. It tapped him on the shoulder and whispered in his ear, but he ignored it.

Suppressing these thoughts the best he could, he ventured farther into the dense unlit forest. A slight chill ran up his spine as he heard a faint howl in the distance. It faded away with the wind that swayed the trees, which grew intense and then faint again, and then much more intense, before fading completely to silence. The occasional crescendos of the chorus of nature put Leo at ease in the sea of his thought, encompassing him, calming him.

"Man, it's cold," Willie muttered, folding his arms tightly over his chest, shivering, walking stiffly.

Leo shrugged. "Not really. It feels . . . warm."

Willie gave him a playful nudge, cracking a cold, frozen smile that was stiff from the chilly night air. "Yeah, well . . . to you. You've always got that jacket on. I bet you still wouldn't even take it off if you were literally standing on the sun."

Willie laughed at his own joke before returning to his shivering, silent state.

Leo rolled his eyes.

It was a long while before either of them found any decent pieces of wood, scanning the ground constantly, searching desperately. Several minutes passed. The two decided to split up to look. By the time they finished searching, it was completely dark out, the long-gone retired sun taking all of its warmth with it.

Willie emerged slowly from the dark forest cradling many pieces of thick, dry wood he had found. He returned to the campsite, dumping the wood into the fire pit, which he would light later. Day was sitting near it on a collapsed log, stirring impatiently but managing to crack a smile. Her smile faded slowly, the confusion in her bulging blue eyes becoming more and more apparent. A wave of worry distorted her warm face, washing it away, taking her smile with it.

"Where's Leo?" she asked him, her eyes wide with panic.

Willie looked at her, confused.

"I thought he came back here. We split up. I . . . I don't know where he could've gone."

Day sprang up, following Willie back into the woods. They ran as fast as they could, glancing through the trees and undergrowth in the darkness, every shape and sound blurring together.

"Leo!" Willie shouted, his desperation growing more and more intense.

The two continued shouting their friend's name as their legs carried them farther and farther away from the deserted campsite. They both came to a halt when they reached a clearing. Willie panted, his heart thumping loudly in his ears. He sat down, resting his head in his hands. He sighed.

"Day, this is all my fault. It was my idea to have us split up."

Just as she was about to respond, she saw a small shuddering movement in the distance, large enough to be seen but miniscule enough to possibly go unnoticed. She caught another fleeting glimpse of the movement and started to run toward it, with Willie trailing behind, jogging lightly. When they got closer, the movements ceased and they were able to see that it was a figure—Leo. They broke out into a quick-paced run, all of their worry washing away with the sight of him in the distance.

"Leo!" Willie shouted. "What are you doing?"

Leo stopped moving but didn't respond. His back was turned. He was silent, standing there stiffly, his limp arms dangled against his sides.

A few seconds passed and Leo still didn't react to his friends' presence. Something was wrong. With shaking hands, he tried once more to get his attention. He gripped Leo's shoulder tightly.

"Leo?" he whispered, his hushed voice trembling along with the leaves in the trees being blown by the now-intensifying wind. Day stood behind him, silent.

Frustrated, Willie grabbed both of Leo's shoulders, whipping him around entirely so that he was facing him. He gasped in shock and immediately let go of his friend.

Leo's eyes were glazed over, almost completely colorless, unblinking, unmoving. His head lay limp, drool dribbling down his face, the thick droplets hitting the ground like foaming rain. Willie stared at him in shock, unaware of what to do, other than stand there hoping something would happen—*anything*—that could fix this. Willie became frustrated, shaking Leo harder and harder. Nothing worked. He couldn't hear anything over the sound of his beating heart, his temples throbbing, accompanied by his sweaty hands trembling.

"Leo, please . . ."

His voice trailed off when he noticed a single slip of paper fall from Leo's limp fingers. The paper looked to be very old—the edges were worn and rolled in on themselves. It was yellowed with age and had several tears near the edges, making the crumpled paper appear more weathered than it was.

Willie bent over to reach for it hesitantly. This made him feel extremely uneasy, even though it was only a mere slip of paper.

Leo continued to stand idly by, his eyes staring straight ahead, his pupils extremely tiny, almost to the point of nonexistence. His stillness was unnatural—never once did he stir, or blink, or even draw a breath. He appeared as though he had been stopped in time, frozen, unaware of himself or anything at all.

As soon as Willie's fingertips brushed against the slip of paper, he drew back immediately. Small burns were beginning to form all over his fingers, turning into boils. He winced in pain, his eyes shut tight in intense agony.

As soon as this happened, Leo gasped loudly and began coughing. He looked up at them, dazed. Day and Willie both stared at him, wide-eyed but relieved.

"What the heck, Leo, what happened?"

Leo shrugged off all of their questions, ignoring them as he noticed Willie's charred fingertips.

"Whoa, what happened to *you?*" he asked, taking Willie's hands to observe them closer, his wavering voice matching his extreme trepidation and incertitude.

Trembling, Willie pointed to the paper he had let float back down to the ground. "Th-th-the paper—it . . . burned me."

Leo followed his gaze. He bent over and scooped it up. "What, this paper?"

Astonished, Willie watched as nothing seemed to happen to Leo. He didn't wince. When he picked it up, he was unaffected.

"Yeah," Willie said quietly.

"So, what's the big deal? I don't see how this burned you. It's just . . . paper," Leo responded, observing the paper, holding it loosely in both hands. He turned the palm-sized paper over, squinting. He brought the paper closer to his face and adjusted his glasses. "There's something written here."

Willie and Day looked on as Leo turned the weathered paper so they could see it, using the light of the moon to try and read it.

Which one will think the loudest? They will win—until they, too, inevitably conform.

Willie narrowed his eyes, glaring down at the paper. Day looked up at him, appearing almost expectant of an answer. The silence was dense, and engulfed the trio in discomfort. Without warning, Leo let the paper flutter to the ground, and started walking away, making his way back through the clearing.

When Willie glanced down to his throbbing hands, it looked as though nothing had happened. There was no sign that the burns had ever existed. He was, however, still in immense pain.

He trailed behind Leo as they made their way through the gap in the dense forest. He could have sworn he saw his father peering at them through the pines, his bulbous eyes emphasized by the moonlight, as well as the slightest hint of a smirk. When Willie turned around again, the figure was gone. He held his fingers out in front of him, rubbing them together, wishing for any physical hint of the pain he was feeling. He cried out in pain as they rubbed together as Leo walked farther and farther away from them.

Day hesitantly walked closer to Willie, taking his hands in hers, but he winced and pulled away.

"Day, wha-what happened to my h-hands?"

She studied them gently. "There's . . . nothing here." She raised her eyebrows, perplexed .

"But you saw it, right?"

"Yeah, your hands were burned pretty bad."

The pain was subsiding, but Willie's heart was still racing, pounding harder than ever. The two continued to lag behind Leo as they all made their way back to the campsite.

CHAPTER TWELVE

Payphone

When they made it out of the depths of the woods, Willie was shocked to find that the pain from his burns had disappeared. He was now in a better mood—giddy even.

He sat down near the fire pit and pulled out a small whittling knife from the burlap bag he packed, took the flattest piece of wood he could find, and began skillfully carving a small hole in the center.

Leo looked on in awe as Willie picked up a stick, held it between his palms, and inserted it into the hole he had made in the slab of wood.

Willie began twirling the stick around, faster and faster, until smoke appeared. After a few more seconds, there was fire.

Willie smirked. "Friction." He laughed, turning to his friends. He tossed more leaves and twigs into the pit, feeding the expanding fire.

The light it emitted flickered on and off, casting a warm glow on the kids' faces as they sat around the orange beacon, facing each other. The stillness of the hot, humid air and the crackling fire brought about an unbearable silence. Willie dug his feet into the dirt, Leo pulled out his sketchbook, and Day watched him sketch the scene of the trees behind their tent. The fire cast a warm glow onto the tent, making the setting look like it was from a picture book—warm yet mysterious.

Eventually, Willie looked up from the ground, the barely noticeable smirk on his face shaded by the shadows draped across his face.

"I have a scary story," he said quietly, smiling. Day rolled her eyes. Mockingly, Willie rolled his eyes as well. "Come on, it's good, 'cause it's a true story," he said, adding suspense to his already overly dramatic voice.

His two friends leaned in to listen. Willie sat across from

the two, his glowing green eyes peeking at the two from over the dancing wisps of flame. Willie began, lowering his voice, "It was a cold, winter night, on Christmas Eve. I couldn't wait for the next day—I was certain I had gotten exactly what I had asked for that year. I was sleeping soundly until . . . it began. There was a horrible creaking noise coming from downstairs. I couldn't tell what it was, but it sounded like a mix between a dying cat and a fork being scratched against a glass plate. I decided to try to go back to sleep, ignoring it. But I couldn't.

"I heard a bang, followed by even more creaks and squeaks, so I decided to just get up to check it out. Hesitantly, I walked down the stairs in the dark. It was coming from outside the door." Willie stopped, looking up for a moment, to glance at his friends. Leo and Day leaned in farther, eager to hear the ending.

"So," he continued, "I turned the doorknob slowly, and *bam!*" he yelled. Leo and Day jumped. "It turned out . . . someone left the screen door open." He threw his head back and laughed, burying his head in his hands.

Day stifled a laugh. "Wow," she muttered sarcastically. Leo groaned.

The three stayed up late, with Willie telling them outrageously bad stories deep into the seemingly perpetual night.

Leo woke up covered in dirt, twigs in his hair, and an unbearably horrible backache. However, he was devasted to be awake.

Recently, being awake was a hell from which he could not climb out of. Every day, as soon as he felt his weak eyelids flicker open, a deep sadness accompanied by an unshakeable fear set in. He was back to the secrets he discovered, back to the deep remorse and regret he felt anytime he remembered that *he* was the one who discovered them, who summoned *himself* into a reality of missing answers. The unknown sucked him in deeper and deeper, into thoughts that led to nowhere, like quicksand.

Squinting with tired eyes, he looked around, realizing he was the first one up. Willie slept on, lying on his back, moving every once in a while, his arms and legs sprawled out. Not too far away lay Day, her body facing away from him.

Leo became bored, lying there on the jagged ground

watching the vanilla-colored sunrise. He decided not to wake Willie and let him wake on his own—waking him was nearly impossible anyways. So, instead, Leo quietly crawled over to Day, with the intent to wake her. He shook her gently, whispering her name. She didn't move. He shook her again, harder, and again, harder and harder.

Something wasn't right. His heart pounded in his throat as he felt the heat of a morbid panic wash over his body. It was clear now, she wasn't breathing. His blood ran cold. With desperate shaking hands, he shook her one last time—nothing.

His heart sank. He turned her over gently, his breath stopping short, snared in his dry throat. Her limp body was sickeningly pale, her eyes lifeless, but wide open. Multiple stab wounds penetrated her delicate, pale neck, the damp blood staining her sky-blue blouse.

Leo looked down at her in panic and disbelief, his tears littering her departed face, the droplets forming constellations across her freckled cheeks.

Leo couldn't look any longer. He buried his head in his hands, bent over, walking away from her, trying to wipe the image of her lifeless oceanic eyes from his mind. *Who did this?* he thought. *And why?*

Leo's sporadic breaths and pacing eventually woke Willie, who was completely unaware of what had happened, eyes flickering open slowly as he emerged gradually from his deep stupor of sleep. Rubbing his eyes, he got up.

Leo couldn't look at him. All he could do was shake his head and point to where Day was, keeping the majority of his face hidden. He wasn't supposed to cry—he'd never allowed himself to cry. *This wasn't supposed to happen.* Nonetheless, hot tears of anger and grief ran down his cheeks as he walked with Willie to the grim scene.

Willie's face fell, his eyes wide. "How?" was all he could say before falling to the ground by her side, shaking. When Willie looked up again, he was scowling, his eyes glazed over, on the verge of shedding tears. He glared at Leo, searching his face for an explanation. "What happened?" he demanded, turning to face Leo completely.

"I-I don't know, I went to wake her, and she was like this," Leo stammered.

"And you didn't see anyone else around?"

"N-no, I didn't."

Willie hesitated a moment, before letting his anger spiral out of control. "Then how do I know it wasn't you?" he snapped.

Leo furrowed his eyebrows, recoiling in shock, astonished at his best friend's words. "What? No. W-why would I—Willie, that's stupid!" he yelled. "Listen to yourself! I would *never* do something like that. I swear to God."

Leo was shocked, afraid, and confused as to why Willie would accuse him of something as horrible as that. It only made him angrier, and made him cry harder. Willie finally came to his senses, wiping the sweat from his forehead. "Leo, look, I'm sorry. I-I wasn't thinking. Really, I'm sorry. I just . . . freaked out."

Leo looked away from him, wiping away his tears with his sleeve. "What're we supposed to do now?" Leo asked him.

Willie took one final look at her frail, helpless form and then turned away to face Leo.

With shaking hands, Willie's footsteps, weak and lifeless, were quickly made desperate. With Leo following closely behind him, he lifted the flap to his father's tent and began to rummage desperately through his things, no longer concerned with the magnitude of noise he was making. It didn't matter anymore—nothing mattered anymore. All he wanted was to disappear.

"Dad!" Willie yelled through hot tears. No answer. Leo looked around frantically, his vision blurring.

"Mr. Everett!" Leo shouted. Nothing.

"Where the hell is he?" Willie muttered quickly, seemingly to himself. He shook his head quickly and continued his search.

Beneath a heap of extra supplies, he managed to find a heavy canvas backpack with many compartments and pockets.

Willie proceeded to frantically dump out all of the contents of the large backpack. Most of it was trash and random assortments of objects, and it fell to the polyester ground of the tent with a medley of different noises created by the vast array of items. Willie quickly scanned the large pile before digging through it wildly, his heart beating in his ears. He could no longer hear anything else, other than his thoughts, screaming at him to hurry up, to leave, to do something, anything.

At the very bottom of the dense pile, he found some coins and breathed a huge sigh of relief. He grabbed a single dirty quarter and stuffed it deep into his pocket. He ran past Leo, who was peering in from the outside of the spacious tent.

Leo once again followed Willie, confused and shaken, out to a clearing similar to the one they were in just hours ago. Like theirs, it was just as desolate and abandoned, with very little differences, except for the fact that there were twice as many picnic benches, which served no purpose to the empty lot—no one would be using them anytime soon, if ever.

Behind the wooden benches with small matching tables in the center were three payphones. Without a second thought, Willie ran up to the closest one and quickly jammed the quarter into the tiny slot. He unlatched the phone from the post and dialed. Nothing happened. Frustrated, Willie slammed the phone back onto the ancient post and buried his head in his hands.

Afraid to speak to Willie in this state, Leo slowly reached into his left pocket and pulled out a small bag of change. He fished around in it for a while before his hand finally surfaced once more, holding a shiny quarter. It nearly slipped out of his shaking, sweaty hands as he handed it to Willie, who took it from him without saying a word.

He tightened his grip on it and began to jog to another payphone. "Come on," he yelled, practically choking out the words. Leo obeyed, stuffing the bag of coins back into his pocket and continuing to trail behind him. Willie uncurled his fingers and slid the quarter into the slot and dialed once more, hoping to get in touch with a police officer or someone of that nature.

Willie could no longer contain his emotions and his eyes began to water, silent tears streaming down his face. *Please work,* he thought, and he thought it so loudly that he could've sworn he had heard the statement from outside of his own head, a desperate cry, a request that he wasn't sure he could fulfill to himself.

His sinking stomach was soothed when he heard someone on the other line pick up. Suddenly, he felt paralyzed with fear, his sweaty hands causing the phone to slip out of his hand, the cord attaching it to the machine suspending it inches above the ground. He couldn't manage to say a single word and fell to the ground slowly, his head in his hands, choking on his tears.

Leo sat down beside him. The two sat in the dry dirt, the gray, heavy sky reminding them of their uncertainty, hopelessness, and terror.

"Willie?"

"What?"

"What are we doing?"

"I-I don't know . . . We need to leave."

Leo swallowed hard and was beginning to feel unsure about Willie's intentions, about what he was thinking. He told himself that there was nothing they could do. The knot of her fate had been tied off in a shockingly unpleasant way, presenting Leo with a sight he wished to never lay his eyes upon ever again—a sight that acted as a catalyst to his morbid panic that began to consume him further and further.

In a way, he felt guilty for what had happened. He knew this wasn't a very rational or valid thought to have, however, he let it take control of his actions from this point on. He wanted to rip out his brain, his eyes. All he could see, painted in the line of his vision vividly before him, was Day's helpless form, unmoving but screaming out in agony, begging for help—his help. He was useless, nothing. Nothing he did stopped him from seeing this scene in his mind, the image a broken record.

He squinted his eyes shut tight. Without warning, he stood up abruptly, startling Willie, who had been dead silent for quite some time, an unnatural sight.

With a hint of anger and desperation in his voice, and with a hint of his now eternally lingering melancholic tone that the two now shared, Leo pulled his friend to his feet. "C'mon Will. We need to leave, now. I can't be here anymore."

Tears flooded down Leo's face, his voice wavering as he spoke, the heavy morning sky that seemed to hang close to the ground making him feel isolated, compressed, unheard.

Willie straightened himself out and the two began running all the way back toward the direction from which they came, away from their attempt at receiving help.

The two ran and didn't stop until they saw all of their

belongings and Willie's father's tent. Willie ran up to the closed, weathered flap of the tent and then stopped.

"I . . . I need to see her. One last time. I can't get the image of her like that out of my head. I need closure," he croaked, almost to himself.

Leo sat down in front the tent, laid down, and turned over on his back, facing away from Willie, and from everything that had happened. He let Willie be, figuring he would want to be left alone in this moment, and so did he. So, he decided he would wait here, closed-eyed, empty-headed, and wait for Willie's return.

In that moment, his impatience took control of him, and thoughts occasionally popped into his head that told him to look for Mr. Everett, or try the payphone again, but he decided against it.

He immediately began drifting in and out of consciousness as sleep grasped him, gripping him tighter and tighter, choking him almost to the point where he had to give in. But the dancing demons in his mind, flickering underneath his eyelids, forced him to stay awake and alert as they tied him to a chair and pried his eyes open, forcing Leo to lay his eyes upon the horrors of earlier events, mere photographs and movies, but real depictions—*very* real. So real he could almost touch them. He held his breath, his heartbeat slowing with the lack of oxygen and demanded his eyes to close again. But all he could see was *her*. It was a perpetual inevitable cycle that had to be witnessed, a cycle from which there was no escape.

But suddenly, there was.

He jumped up off the ground and quickly brought himself to his feet, as a piercing scream sounded from behind him, shattering the bare morning sky.

It was Willie.

CHAPTER THIRTEEN
Unknowing

"Leo? Leo! Come here, hurry!" His shaky voice rang throughout the trees and over the sky, almost putting everything in a prolonged state of immense shock with its level of extreme intensity, never heard through these woods as long as the trees had stood where they did.

He ran as fast as his legs could carry him toward Willie, who continued to cry out to him, his voice manic. Leo tapped him on the shoulder and Willie stopped when he realized Leo was right behind him, who began to look at him, puzzled. Willie pointed over to where they had last seen Day, his trembling finger a clear symptom of his immense terror. In a voice that was almost impossible to hear, Willie whispered to Leo.

"Look," he mumbled, casting his gaze away from the area where he was pointing.

Leo looked out in the direction opposite Willie and shrugged, his glazed eyes full of confusion.

"What? There's nothing there, Willie."

Willie looked back at him, his eyes wide in apparent disbelief.

"Y-yeah, exactly!" he stammered, trying desperately to stifle the panic working its way up his throat. "Sh-she was *right* there—I swear it! Go look for yourself!"

Hesitantly, Leo walked closer to the forbidden space, every step sending chills down his spine, every twig snap pleading with him to turn back. The sheets and the sleeping bag she had been laid on top of were completely free of any sign that something had ever happened here. The ground on which the sheets and layers of fabric sat was untainted by tragedy—unsuspecting dirt was all that remained. Leo looked around frantically, searching for her.

Suddenly, something sitting at the edge of the sleeping bag caught his attention. It was small, blowing faintly in the brisk, chilling wind, which seemed to spawn from nowhere in particular. He squatted down to get a better look at it. It was barely visible in the dull early morning light, unassisted by the lazy sun that shone an almost flickering light, leaving everything with a dull hue, the muted colors practically nonexistent.

Leo grabbed it and turned it over in his hands. It was fabric—no, a small cloth. A piece of material torn from Day's shirt. In the pale light, it was difficult to make out the light-blue color. Leo gasped and tried to contain his worry.

"What's that?" Willie asked him, having been peering silently over Leo's shoulder the whole time.

"It's a torn piece of Day's shirt," Leo responded, his frown turning more and more sour.

Willie grabbed it from him and held it up. "Sure looks like it." As though holding in an immense amount of rage, Willie threw the wilted fabric down in frustration and looked at Leo. "It doesn't matter. It doesn't explain anything. *Anything!*" he shouted, grabbing Leo's shoulders.

Leo stood still and silent. The two stood there for a while, looming over the one place they promised they would never see again, ever. And yet, there they were. A full circle had been completed. Amid the island of silence on which the two resided, many thoughts circled above their heads, which were just incomplete fragments, slight understanding, frustration; confusion. Leo looked up at Willie, someone he had always counted on, someone he could always look to for confidence, for happiness, for . . . a way out.

Willie's tall figure loomed over his head, a weeping willow engulfing him in melancholic pale-yellow auras, the ghost of whom he once was leaving through his eyes. Leo decided he would have this person back—maybe not today, maybe not tomorrow, but someday.

Leo's spinning thoughts pushed him more and more into denial as he began to tell himself small lies. *She's not actually dead. She'll be back soon. Nothing happened. Nothing. Nothing. Nothing. Nothing. Stop. Stop. Stop!* He couldn't keep it inside anymore and began voicing his thoughts, hoping that one statement, just one, would be true.

"Hey, maybe she just . . . went somewhere for a while. She'll be back, right? *Right?*" Willie looked at him angrily, seconds before Leo burst into tears. "Please tell me she's okay! She is, isn't she?"

Willie sighed deep and long before putting both of his hands on Leo's shoulders, forcing Leo to look into his eyes.

His expression was intense, his eyes red and hurt, angry yet vulnerable and broken, tired yet wide awake, his usual easily fathomed emotions now shrouded in mystery. He spoke in a stern, assertive voice.

"Leo. *No.* She is *dead.* We saw her. Please stop. There's nothing we can do."

A single tear dripped from his eye landing hard on the ground, the sound absorbed by the dense nature of their world.

Suddenly, a pair of bright taillights could be seen driving off into the distance near the empty parking lot that held Mr. Everett's car.

The two boys exchanged glances before running after it as fast as they could, curiosity and desperation consuming them. They ran until they felt as though their lungs would burst, their feet slapping the pavement of the parking lot loudly, echoing throughout the dense woods that seemed to absorb all sound as quickly as it received it. When Leo and Willie finally got close enough to the car, they instantly recognized the signature white stripe in the middle and the three sirens positioned an equal distance apart on the top—a police car. They both stopped dead in their tracks, the pieces coming together.

Panting, Willie looked down at Leo, trying his utmost to speak again. "Do . . . Do you think they took Day?"

For once, Leo wasn't the one asking all of the questions.

Although still extremely distraught, Leo found this to be a reasonable theory and was relieved to see that there was no longer a horrific misunderstanding.

"Yeah," he answered confidently as he began to walk back to their clearing. Daybreak was far gone now and afternoon was approaching rapidly.

As Leo walked on, he noticed Willie wasn't following him, and instead continued to watch as the police car drove slowly away, the rocky dirt road shaking the car slightly. He watched as the sun peeked slowly out from beneath the clouds and small droplets of rain began to prickle his skin slightly.

The small buildings in the distance appeared to be instantly covered up by a fog the gentle rain brought down with it from the dewy heavens.

The police car, still slow as ever, finally reached the top of the hill that led out onto the nearly empty street. Willie watched as a bigger chunk of fabric floated through the wind from near the car, seemingly originating from inside of the vehicle. It landed limply on the sidewalk .

He ran up the hill and onto the sidewalk next to the street and grabbed it, his distance from Leo ever increasing, his footsteps heavy and forced. He stretched the fabric out some, only to discover that there was a massive bloodstain in the middle, dry and now turned a dark brown, hardly recognizable as blood—but he knew. He tucked it into his pocket and jogged back to where Leo was, who had stopped walking and stood still, waiting for his friend's return.

When Leo saw him approaching, he turned to face his direction, slouching. Willie dug around in his pocket and pulled out the stained patch of fabric.

"Look what came out of the back window of their car." He held the fabric out for Leo to take, who did, but didn't say a word, and let it flutter to the ground.

"Do you know what this means? They have her," Leo responded emotionlessly.

"Well, yeah, it's not like she could just vanish or something."

There was silence.

Willie led Leo up the steep hill to the road and pointed directly across the street.

"You see that road up there? The one that leads to the main highway?"

Leo nodded.

"Well, they passed it and went that way." Willie pointed to the right.

Leo didn't see what he was getting at, and Willie picked up on this and proceeded to get mildly frustrated with him.

"Leo, there's nothing that way for *miles*! I looked in that direction on our way here. We need to know what they're doing. What if they're—why would they have—why would they carry a dead body out to the middle of nowhere?"

For every statement Willie made, his voice escalated in volume, each word, each syllable sounding more and more crazed by the next. Upon taking note of Willie's drastic change in behavior, Leo had begun to think. Was this how he sounded earlier?

Leo's heart pounded in his chest as he became more and more angry at whoever would do such a horrible thing to someone such as Day, and even more angry over the new emotions he felt because of this, and how Willie was forced to feel.

With that thought, Leo took a deep breath and began talking to Willie, trying his best to maintain a steady tone and remain confident, careful to not start tearing up again.

"Don't worry about it. I'm sure it meant absolutely nothing, and that they're getting to the bottom of it. Let's just focus on getting back home for now, which means figuring out where your dad went."

Willie turned his head and looked down at Leo, wiping the messy, tangled hair out of his face only to reveal intensely red eyes filled with anger and confusion. Willie slammed his hands to his sides loudly, the sound spreading to all sides of the small, rectangular parking lot, springing up from every crack.

"Oh, why does everything in my life have to be so . . . weird and unfair!" he yelled, ripping at his hair. "First, my dad persuaded me to take you guys on this stupid trip, and then you go into the woods and you're all . . . weird and dazed, and then that paper that burned me, and now Day."

Willie sunk to his knees and began sobbing, putting his hands over his ears. Leo reached out to help him up, but Willie shoved his hand away.

"No! Don't," he yelled, curling himself up tighter against the dirty pavement. "Just leave!"

Leo felt the deepest sorrow for him , and it made his own eyes tear up just seeing how much agony Willie was in. He looked back to the clearing that seemed so far away now and Mr. Everett was still nowhere to be found. Leo yanked on his arm.

"Come on! Let's go home."

"No. Leave me alone. Go without me. I don't care."

"I'm not gonna leave you here."

Leo sat down next to Willie without saying a word. He would

wait as long as he had to, despite the hot sun slowly burning a hole through him and the boiling pavement making his legs feel as though they were on fire. He wasn't going to leave Willie here, and he wasn't going to leave him ever.

It seemed as though hours went by, and Leo was left alone with his thoughts. He decided to let Willie be and give him time to think about things for himself, which seemed to be going well, because every once in a while, Willie would speak.

And finally, after what seemed like many uneventful eternities in the blistering, desert-like heat, Willie, in a dry hushed voice, spoke six glorious words: "Are you ready to go now?"

With that, Leo got up quickly and brushed the dirt from his shorts. Once more, he extended his hand to help Willie up, and this time, he took it firmly.

Willie began running back to the clearing, away from the parking lot, from his uncertainty, while Leo eagerly followed behind him.

When they approached the clearing, the boys came to discover that Mr. Everett was now back, evidenced by the loud stirring that moved the tent slightly, which could be heard in the distance when their footsteps fell silent.

"Where the hell has he been?" Willie muttered.

"Wait here," Willie commanded Leo, as he reluctantly began walking over to the area where the three of them had slept that night, gathering all of their things and walking at a brisk pace back over to Leo, handing him his belongings without a word. All was quiet except for the slight occasional rustling of leaves, the snapping of twigs, and the chirping of birds mocking them, taunting them.

Suddenly, Willie began sprinting toward his father's tent, desperate to be as far away from this place as he could. The fact that Willie was standing in the exact same spot as he had been when he found Day sent him into a blind panic that brought tears to his eyes and quickened his already-labored breathing.

Willie got closer to the spacious tent, practically ripping the flap off when he reached it, then climbed inside, surprised to find that his dad was present, appearing asleep, as he was lying down flat on his back, his usual glazed, empty eyes wide open.

Willie sighed and began shaking him frantically. "Come on, we need to go."

Mr. Everett raised his head slightly and peered at Leo through the opening in the tent, then at Willie.

Willie backed slowly out of the tent as his father slowly emerged, clumsily, into the sun. Willie groaned with impatience and began packing up the tent among other items by himself while Leo looked on in a strange yet familiar realization. Willie couldn't quite recognize it, nor did he know what this realization was exactly.

CHAPTER FOURTEEN
Welcome

Day slowly opened her aching eyes and glanced around. She couldn't see a thing within the infinite black abyss that dwelled on all sides of her, swallowing her up.

Feebly, she attempted to look down at the mysterious contraption that seemed to hold her in place, but her head wouldn't move. She quickly came to the realization that, no matter how hard she tried, she could not move a single muscle in her body, not even a tiny bit. Her face felt numb. She felt powerless, drained, stripped of all her senses, only to suffer silently, alone in the dark.

A wave of panic spread throughout her body. She wanted to scream, but her voice was permanently stifled, rid of sound. She couldn't get it to make a sound—not even the slightest fractal of a sound was generated. Her heart raced in her chest; the only thing she could seem to hear in this moment was her thoughts.

All she knew was that she needed to leave this place. Her last memory was a haze, a confusing and dark haze that led to a completely unfathomable outcome. Her surroundings, completely shrouded in darkness, intimidated her in an ominous and mysterious way, sending her deeper into a blind panic that could not be soothed.

She closed her eyes and tried to calm down. Her last memory was . . . she couldn't remember. All she could see was small, brief flashes of a possibly significant event, yet all she knew was that it was fatal.

She saw herself, backing away hurriedly from . . . people, concealed to the eye, cloaked in the night, apparitions of stealth. There was no sound in her memory, only the intense pounding of her heartbeat in her ears. There was a struggle. Then, she remembered not moving, not running—she couldn't. Her breathing ceased to carry on as she surrendered to the mysterious beings that proceeded to roughly toss her away into a box of some sort. Helpless and unmoving, she was thrown into the back of a car and hurried away, which was all she remembered.

Day started to grow immensely frustrated with herself, as she still couldn't even come close to beginning to understand what any of that could mean or what it would have to do with her being *here*—wherever "here" was.

Suddenly, bright blinding lights came on, followed by a loud crashing noise, as one of the giant light fixtures tied poorly to the industrial ceiling plummeted to the floor and shattered, flooding glass shards into every possible direction. The remaining lights fastened to the ceiling flickered, emitting a muted yellow light, and revealed a vast, clean, empty room with white bare walls and no windows, except for one, whose length stretched out the entirety of the blank wall before her.

In this moment, Day realized she *could* move, as she had begun to try to progressively relax each limb and concentrate on bringing each to life. She lifted her arms out in front of her, wiggling her fingers, and turning her shaking hands over. She could now feel the immense amount of sweat that covered her and plastered her hair to her head, her delicate curls suffocated. She looked down only to realize that she had been contained by a tall, metal chair with straps attached to it, accompanied by a harness, which, to her surprise, no longer contained her.

Day jumped from the chair and onto the ground landing on her feet, hard. She winced as the pain shot up through both of her legs, the surge of sudden suffering motivating her to find a way out even further. She turned around out of curiosity and was startled to discover that the wall behind the chair was completely covered in full-length mirrors, stretching from floor to ceiling. She stepped closer to look.

To her surprise, there were dark bags under her eyes. Her whole body appeared weaker, more frail than she had recalled. The clothing she had been wearing was gone, replaced with a dark burgundy jumpsuit made of thick corduroy-like material, complete with a large metal zipper on the front. It fit loosely against her body. She felt the coarse material, confused, but too dazed to question it, or anything. There were no questions— only panic and fear, and the overwhelming urge to *get out*.

In the midst of her trepidation, she had begun to remember

her wound. She distinctly remembered the areas where she recalled it happening, running her hands over her chest and neck, curiously feeling no pain. She frantically unzipped the bulky outfit and felt underneath the thin white blouse that lied beneath.

The wounds were still there, unchanged. Day inspected her neck and it was the same. She felt as though she was going to be sick as the sides of her vision began to fade to black. Her knees felt weak and she could no longer find the strength to hold herself up as she dropped to the ground, her grip on the mirrored wall slipping.

Her whole body developed an unbearably intense tingling sensation that made her want to rip her skin off and be rid of all the swarming bugs that buzzed rapidly beneath the pulsating layers. She turned around to face the wall with the window and she caught a glimpse of someone, or something—she wasn't sure.

The crawling feeling grew more intense as the dim lights above her appeared to grow brighter, revealing the figure staring at her from the window, unmoving—completely still, dead silent.

She shut her eyes tightly and the sensation ceased to exist as quickly as it had overcome her. When she opened her eyes again, the feeling returned with more intensity than before.

Day stumbled over to the window, longing to get a better look at whoever the figure was, even though she knew she shouldn't. But there didn't appear to be any apparent means of exit within the vast space, so she decided to push her paranoid thoughts away and continue drawing closer, and closer.

The figure remained unnaturally still as Day continued to come closer, her shoulders tensing, her jaw clenched. The crawling feeling, she noticed, was now more aggressive than ever, and Day could almost see her skin buzzing, moving up and down at an alarmingly quick pace. The person, was clad in a robe, made of an assortment of many different types of fabrics of variated, but dull, colors. The face was not visible, as it was covered by a very old animal mask, which appeared to resemble a lizard of some sort.

Amid the thick silence, Day could now hear faint whispers

and voices coming from the room behind the window, in which the Lizard stood. She stared at the Lizard, confused, not daring to move a muscle.

A group of people emerged from the mirrored wall through a disguised narrow doorway that Day had not noticed before. A dozen other mask-wearers emerged, each sporting the same one as the man in the window.

Day whimpered and cowered in fear as they all began to stand around her in V-formation, as if this was an event that had been carefully planned. While the man looking in the window from the other room monitored, the group began to close in on her slowly, every one of their silent footsteps providing a bridge into a certain unknown fate.

Paralyzed in fear, she allowed herself to slowly sink back to the cold cement floor. She couldn't speak, nor could she find the strength to move, to do anything. As much as she wanted to be out of this room—which seemed to grow hotter and hotter by the minute—and never see these people ever again, she couldn't move.

A short gasp escaped her throat as she felt a sharp pain radiate down her upper back and move down her spine. Her whole body went limp and her hands fell lifelessly to the ground, numbed once more. Her sight began to fail her as everything faded slowly to black, the sharp ringing in her ears growing more intense and the quickening of her breathing barely heard over the noise.

The cloaked people who surrounded her began to back up quickly as the man she recognized from the window emerged from the hidden doorway. Approaching her slowly, his gloved, unexposed hands were held behind his back. He bent down to her level, his hidden face almost directly touching hers.

Day wanted nothing more than to disappear, the petrifying silence and occasional whispers making her heart beat out of her chest. She felt as though she was floating, her numb body practically lifeless. It felt like she wasn't lying down at all, but rather, held up by four strings, one for each limb, or laid down flat on an invisible table, towering high into the air. Day couldn't feel a thing when the man's quick yet steady fingers lifted her chin up, forcing her to stare at the ceiling, which seemed to be closing in on her slowly.

The man untied his plentiful robes, revealing a plain-looking denim leisure suit with a brown jacket and an enamel-pin nametag that read DR. CLOVER, complete with matching pants, which fit strangely on his slender, lanky body. He then proceeded to strip his face of the foolish mask, disclosing an asymmetrical smirk that seemed to take up most of his narrow face. He hoisted Day to her feet, roughly draping her over his shoulder and carrying her through the mirrored door.

The room that its ominous mouth opened up to was just as uncanny as the one she had woken up in—it was completely silent, and judging by the echoing footsteps of the others trailing behind Dr. Clover, the room was quite large and extremely empty.

Once again, Day felt as though she were going to faint, but just before she drifted off into another unavoidable, unintentional repose, she heard faint mumbling erupt into laughter with unknown context.

"Be quiet!" the doctor yelled loudly, banging on the wall to get the masked crowd to cease their noise.

Day opened her eyes with a start, dancing around wildly. The man looked over his shoulder quickly to face her. Day looked at him, paralyzed, her eyes wide with terror.

The man chuckled softly before pulling a nearby cord to switch on the lights above their heads, blinding her, as she drifted out of consciousness.

"Welcome," he whispered softly into her ear.

CHAPTER FIFTEEN

Letters

The car ride back felt strange, the atmosphere heavy, a chip in a fragile china plate; Willie and Leo felt odd to be leaving without someone they arrived with. Mr. Everett said nothing, responding to their frantic statements with a stare that seemed to look behind their eyes.

Leo couldn't focus, his thoughts making the quiet, gently humming car seem loud, a swimming carousel of dismay circling about his tired head. He felt tired, sick, and guilty. The fact that he was uncertain as to why he was feeling so many emotions at once only made him more tired.

Mr. Everett adjusted the flimsy overhead mirror, and Leo caught his deep, empty gaze, which seemed to be taunting him, mocking him; he could've sworn he had seen him smirk. Leo averted his gaze out the window, staring on at the heavy, overcast sky, the dark clouds descending from above and dancing across the vast, empty street, not a care in the world, unaware of the messy, dismal haze they had begun to spread across the flat, grassy plains that seemed to stretch forever and ever.

Neither Leo nor Willie spoke a word the entire time, muted by what they had seen. Several minutes went by, which seemed to translate into hours, then days, months, years, millennia. Willie's father returned them both to the present, reaching out a delicate, almost lifeless hand, tuning the radio slowly. Leo clutched the now rolled-up sleeping bag he had brought with him tightly against his chest, and set his backpack, seemingly heavier now, onto the minimal space available on the floor of the weathered car, pulling his legs up and setting them on top of the stuffed bag. Leo couldn't prevent himself from fidgeting, and it was driving him mad; all he wanted was to sleep so his thoughts could be at ease, so he wouldn't have to think about . . . her, and how drained and helpless she looked, and how he couldn't do anything to help her because it was too late, and how he would never, *ever* stop thinking about it. And the images played in a perpetual reel in his head, over and over and over, each interpretation of what he had seen even more exaggerated than the last.

He tightened his grip on the sides of his pants, rubbing his eyes firmly with his fingers, tensed in extreme agitation. He found himself thinking hard about everything, *everything* around him. He glanced over at Willie to make sure he wasn't watching, and slowly reached into his back pocket, taking out the weathered strip of paper Willie had found in the woods. He felt its worn, yellowed ridges, desperately trying to feel the same burning sensation Willie had felt, along with the mysterious blisters that seemed to vanish as quickly as they were inflicted upon his calloused fingertips. His anxiety was perpetuated when he began to truly notice how strange it felt in the vehicle without the presence of Day. Everything was exactly the same: the atmosphere, the surroundings. But somehow, everything felt different now: a school at night, an empty city. He longed for all of this to be over with, or, better yet, he longed for none of this to have ever happened.

He continued to look out the window, hoping to catch a glimpse of something he recognized—a street name, a sign, a tree. Nothing. Everything was just as unfamiliar as when they were travelling here. He glanced around again—at Mr. Everett, at Willie. The two felt tense due to the fact that the barely animated man hadn't even reacted to the fact that someone was missing. He hadn't said a word yet. Now that he thought about it, Leo had never even heard Mr. Everett speak, which he considered a good thing, especially if his speech matched his discourteous behavior, which was only expressed through small gestures and unbecoming facial expressions that Leo and Willie himself found offensive.

He directed his gaze towards Willie, who hadn't really moved since he had gotten into the car. He sat with his arms crossed, his hands draped over his thighs. He tapped his foot rapidly as if in extreme anticipation, or anxiousness, or both—Leo couldn't really tell. His long, thick hair, tangled and exaggerated by the humidity that hung low in the air, covered the majority of his face on the left side, and from Leo's perspective, his entire face was almost completely absorbed by his hair, a thick, messy forest, a reserve of which no one else was allowed to cast their eyes upon.

Leo was a hitchhiker within his own mind, desperate to find a way out, but desperate to never allow himself to trust anyone, ever again; not after what had happened. He knew Willie was looking at him, and he wanted so badly to talk to him, but he just didn't know what to say, and he knew that Willie probably didn't either. He felt way too comfortable smothering himself in his guilt that resonated within his head and writhing in his own melancholic thoughts to emerge back out of the place where he had been sent to. However, deep in the dark corners of his heart, he wanted to return, and to forget. His internal monologue was filled with contradictions, with emotions he couldn't piece together, so he left them alone and allowed his sullen head to rest against the cold car window.

Rain had begun to trickle down from the heavens, beginning with a few pokes on the roof of the car before breaking out into a jarring cascade of water droplets, pouring down in countless numbers, filling the silent ride with the illusion of imaginary conversation. The sky cried their tears as the never-ending nightmare ride back dragged on, which seemed to move at an even slower pace as they drew closer to home. With that in mind, Leo allowed himself to fall asleep, turning his head sideways, allowing it to rest on the sleeping bag he was holding. Although it was not one of the most comfortable positions to sleep in, Leo found it sufficient, and fell asleep almost immediately.

He awoke to Willie tapping him lightly from outside of the car, which was parked outside his familiar cul-de-sac. He got up slowly, unbuckled his seatbelt, and climbed clumsily out of the car before reaching back in and grabbing his things. It was night, and the crickets were chirping loudly, filling the soggy night with shrill summer noise. Willie walked Leo to his door in silence, afraid that the slightest of comments would trigger an inevitable emotional landslide that would leave the two of them even more shaken than they were initially. With tired, shaking fingers, Leo reached underneath the wide mat in front of the door and took the key that was hidden beneath. He opened the door slowly and then stepped inside, turning his back to the outdoors. He began to shut the door.

"Leo, wait!"

Leo was startled to hear a voice for the first time in what seemed like forever, his perpetual isolation shattered by two singular words. He turned back around to face Willie once more, waiting to hear what his friend was going to say.

Willie looked down at his feet, digging them into the rough pavement, creating a resounding, scratching sound that rang out in every direction in the large neighborhood.

"I'm sorry," he said in a hushed voice, "for . . . putting you through all of that."

Leo looked at him, puzzled.

"H-how is any of this *your* fault?" he asked timidly.

There was a long silence.

"Because, Leo, I was the one who convinced you guys to come, and my dad wanted to do it so bad, and . . ."

Willie's voice trailed off.

"Willie, it doesn't matter. That had nothing to do with you. I know it's hard, but just . . . try not to think about it like that."

Willie nodded his head solemnly in agreement.

"You're right. You're right a lot, Leo."

"I know. Good night."

With that, Leo shut the door and turned the kitchen light on, revealing the silhouette of Chester sitting in the parlor, reading from the paper. He was shrouded in darkness, his only source of light the faint glow of the swollen moon filtering in through the slits in the blinds in the window he was sitting next to. When Leo noticed his father's lanky silhouette, he was extremely startled, and jumped a little, nearly dropping the key.

"Hello, Leo," he said without turning his head to look up.

Leo's heart raced. It had been . . . a while since he had talked to him like this. It felt normal almost.

"H-hello, Father," he answered hesitantly. He walked slowly towards the stairs, hoping to escape the uncomfortable silence that lingered. Suddenly, he felt an immense guilt developing in his stomach; he'd never remembered to tell him or Mary where he was going, and he had been gone for a whole day. Leo shrugged it off; Chester didn't seem to care, as usual, and he assumed that his mother was already gone for the evening. He continued to walk upstairs, floating upwards on quick, hurried footsteps that carried him away from everything that made him feel . . . odd.

When he finally reached his room, he undressed immediately and climbed into an oversized old T-shirt and sweatpants, diving under the covers of his bed, desperate for sleep to take him away from this nightmare of a day. After having been situated for quite some time, Leo realized he felt strange; he felt extremely tired, so tired he could hardly move, but every time he closed his eyes, he just couldn't get them to stay that way. They would dance around underneath the cloak of his heavy eyelids, flitting about in every direction until his eyes were forced open, demanding that he stare out into the quiet, uneventful darkness of his room. This happened countless times, and eventually Leo realized he had lost the battle.

Frustrated, he rubbed his eyes and sat up, slouching, his head in his hands. Suddenly, his palms became sweaty, and his heart had begun to race—his thoughts about earlier were returning, even though he thought he had gotten rid of them forever, or at least just reduced them to tiny fractals whose smaller pieces belonged to a bigger picture—a picture he wanted to avoid, a picture he never wanted to see again. But it was too late, because that tiny, singular acknowledgement to his own thought about thinking about her brought on an unbearable, choking panic. He could still see her vividly: still, forever. There was no fixing this. It was over, wasn't it?

His fruitless attempts at self-soothing proved more harmful than just facing it and thinking about it. He gripped the blanket that covered his legs tightly with his hands and closed his eyes, attempting to transport himself to anywhere . . . *anywhere* else besides his own mind. He tried imagining himself in a vast meadow, where the wind tousled his hair gently, and he tried to imagine he was in space, drifting past Andromeda and Messier 82, far beyond the Milky Way, never to return. He floated past the billions of freckled stars that surrounded him on all sides, engulfing him in a bright, beautiful, and silent home. However, these desperate attempts did not work at all, and Leo found himself just as hopeless as he was before.

He only knew one way to solve this: he drowsily stumbled off of his bed and walked over to the window that sat in front of his desk, cracking it open slightly. The brisk night air smelled sweet, the damp moisture lingering in the air still, surviving from earlier, which to him seemed like lifetimes ago. However, the heavy air laced with dew was among one of the only pieces of evidence that it had even happened, along with the occasional flashes of lightning, igniting random clouds with bright lights in various tones, snapping pictures of the melancholic feeling that continued to linger long after the storm was over. The rolling thunder in the distance, which seemed to get extremely close but then back away timidly , added to the themed soundscape of despair, the sky reaped of its plentiful tears.

Leo opened the window a little bit further and slid through slowly, careful not to make even the slightest of sounds. Finally, he was out. Carefully, he rested the soles of his feet onto the thin windowsill and began to climb all of the windows, careful not to slip and tumble down off the slippery, narrow edges.

When he reached the roof, he lay down, spreading his limbs out entirely, staring up at a starless sky. He held his hands out in front of him, tracing the creases in the palm of his left hand with his right. The night sky was a blank canvas, an empty thought. But just this once, to ease his mind, he could pretend that the stars were all there. The wind blew through the trees that engulfed him with a great force, soothing his racing heart, drying his sweaty forehead, calming his troubled mind. Out here, he finally felt like he could understand himself and why he felt this way. He searched inside himself for any hints, and realized there was no straightforward answer. He decided that all he had to do was realize he wasn't hopeless and tell himself that eventually his pain would ease—but not tonight. Tonight, he could cry. Tonight, he could think about her. When he allowed himself to do so, he realized that doing the very thing he didn't want to do was the thing he needed to do, and with that, his racing thoughts allowed him to rest, to sleep beneath the starless sky, to dream of . . . nothing—cold, empty nothing.

Leo awoke to a strange vision, which he was uncertain was a vision or a part of real life. Leo felt his whole body tense up, and then go numb altogether. The door to his bedroom had been opened ajar, revealing the thick, dark abyss that lurked outside his door—an enigmatic mass that only existed at night, a world he would never dare go near. However, tonight, it was different. Leo narrowed his eyes, squinting as hard as he could into the barren darkness; it was no use, and he couldn't catch even the smallest of glimpses of movement like he had seen before.

He reluctantly glanced at the slightly open door again, and he felt his spine tingle as he saw a flash of light drift by. He sat up quickly at the edge of his bed, a wave of panic descending downwards from the top of his head, making his body feel hot. Cold beads of sweat formed on his forehead as he slowly allowed himself to slide off the foot of the bed and approach the door with delicate, soundless footsteps. He walked as quietly as he could across the wooden floorboards before allowing a small, quick gasp to escape from his throat when one of the old boards creaked beneath his weight.

The dead silence of the still, night air only made his heart pound harder in his chest, in his ears. He tried to think of nothing and concentrated only on holding his breath. The walk to the door seemed so long now. His whole body tried to pull him away, but his mind allowed him to do nothing besides go through with what he had planned: investigate. He pushed all thoughts aside and hurriedly ran to the door, stopping abruptly when he reached the part where it had been opened slightly. He swallowed hard and stared out into the silent darkness, which seemed to be staring back at him.

Suddenly, the light was back: a figure, a woman, made of . . . light. Leo backed away rapidly, falling backward before running to take refuge within the sheets of his bed.

Wide-eyed, he remained sitting up, allowing his thoughts to engulf him like the bed sheets he had draped over his shaking shoulders. He felt divided; he wanted to believe he hadn't seen anything at all—he wanted to believe that more than anything. But there was still the lingering thought that lived at the very front of his mind that nagged him, poked him, screamed at him, telling him he did, he did, *he did.*

Leo glanced around the darkened room, his eyes searching for something, *anything* that would allow him to forget such an enigma. After a lot of barely awake sitting and doing nothing, he soon realized that he was . . . mad at himself, mad for letting himself believe such a thing could really exist. It didn't, and he decided he would allow himself to believe this, as it was the only thing there to soothe his overactive mind, to get rid of the singular hyper-fixation he had seemed to develop in less than half an hour.

Feeling numb, he allowed himself to sink down further until he was lying down again. He let his muscles relax, his fists uncurl, his jaw unclench. But nothing would stop his mind from expressing at least *some* concern, so, in order to maintain his state of bliss, he made a deal with himself: he would allow his eyes to wonder over to the door periodically, but he would not be permitted to think about what he thought he saw. He calmly lay there, thinking about only not-thinking about what troubled him, which, while contradictory, soothed him more than anything else he had tried.

Just as he had begun to feel tiredness take its inevitable grip on his eyes, he saw it again, but this time, it lingered, and began to open the door wider and wider until it was open entirely, revealing the empty, long corridor hidden somewhere in the darkness. Once again, Leo couldn't move nor make a sound. He looked on in horror as the figure started to become more human-like than it already appeared. The body, which seemed to be made of light, turned black and blended in with the areas of his room that were unlit by the moon. The figure took on an even more pronounced shape of a woman, no longer a silhouette, or a mere figment of his deceiving imagination. She approached Leo, slowly, silently, as if she was hurting. Her shaky, forced footsteps led Leo to believe that she was . . . weak. He wanted to back away, to hide, to jump out of the window; anything to be rid of what was playing out in front of him. She continued to walk towards him, hunched over, gripping her stomach tightly as if she were in intense pain, which he concluded to be true. Nevertheless, he was terrified, but he couldn't look away as her pained, shuffling footsteps grew louder, closer. Her outstretched arms reached out to him as far as they could, pain in every desperate movement. Leo backed up as far as he could, but it was no use. Suddenly, he felt a sensation of cold wash over his body, which was centered around the middle of his chest. He was frozen in fear, lost in a haze of confusion that quickly spread throughout his body, the heat making the cold in the center of his chest tingle and itch with a ferocity that he had never before experienced.

When he found that he could move again, he took quick, forced breaths, which seemed to use up every ounce of energy he had. His shifting eyes tried their utmost to avoid the form-less woman reaching out in front of him, unmoving. He looked down to the center of his chest, the cold sensation spreading throughout his body. The woman's shadowed hand was reach-ing straight through the center of his body limply, while the rest of her body remained completely stiff and seemingly lifeless. Leo tried to break free, but he found that he couldn't. He couldn't move any part of his body at all; he couldn't breathe. He sat on his bed, wide-eyed, the edges of his vision a kaleidoscope, fading to dark colors and meaningless shapes. Everything was shiny. He felt as though his mind was beginning to . . . close in on itself, to sleep while he was still awake. Whatever was hap-pening, there was nothing he could do.

Before he could close his eyes and embrace his seeming-ly eternal process of demise, everything stopped. His body felt normal, and he no longer felt the woman's presence. His eyes opened quickly, squinting around the dark room—nothing was there. *Nothing.*

Leo furrowed his brow in frustration and sighed. He felt as though nothing was real anymore, and if it was, he had no way of telling. With shaking, weak footsteps, he walked over to his bookshelf, and began pulling books out from the bottom shelf; he, however, wasn't set on looking for anything in particular, but was more preoccupied with the idea of doing something, *anything* to take his mind off of what had just happened to him. Just the feeling of moving about and doing something other than . . . nothing, paralyzed on his bed for what seemed like hours, was an immense relief to him that soothed his aching mind.

He stared down at the messy pile of books that he made, each of the titles providing no interest to him whatsoever. He picked up a large hardcover book, removing the jacket before taking the book back to his bed. He sat at the edge of the bed and cracked the spine of the thin book. It hadn't occurred to him that he had never once opened it up before, as he fre-quented the part of his bookshelf where he pulled it from quite often. It was filled with detailed drawings of star maps with descriptions. As he flipped the pages, he realized that he wasn't really looking, but rather staring into the printed images, not making anything of them. His mind was beginning to wander as he stared into the circles filled with seemingly endless amounts of tiny dots surrounded by words, all forced into a tiny space, barely legible, reflecting his internal monologue. He began skimming the paragraphs under the diagrams, however unaware of what he was reading, but still managing to be distracted, which was appreciated.

He flipped through the thin book for quite a while before gently tossing it away from him and sprawling himself out onto the floor, staring up at the textured ceiling, which seemed to be spinning. However, Leo decided that he would not give in to his heavy eyelids, which yearned for sleep, and his fatigued body, which longed to stop moving around. The last thing he wanted to do was sleep; just the thought of it sent him into an extreme internal panic. He felt extremely nauseous and hot, as the large room had suddenly begun to feel like a cage with no air, suffocating him slowly.

He quickly came to the realization that all he could think about anymore was Day. He saw her over and over and over again. Everything was . . . chaotic, his thoughts an eclectic collection of everything he didn't want to think about. He felt himself losing control, and started to panic, trapped in an unfathomable worry, a worry that he couldn't understand, a worry about things that he could not control. He swallowed hard, got up, and began to pace around his dark room, trying his hardest to focus only on inhaling and exhaling, ignoring the plea of his burning, throbbing eyes to sleep. He couldn't listen, and he refused to give in to this desire. He was far too afraid of what he might see if he did.

Hours passed. Leo tiredly walked over to the window behind his desk, his footsteps heavy. He slowly climbed up onto the wobbling desk and cracked open the window, just wide enough for him to slide through, and sat on the windowsill, letting his feet hang over the edge, hitting the exterior of the house gently. He sat, unmoving, for what seemed like a brief moment, a fleeting blink, a turn of the head. His eyes burned and were heavy as he stared out into the sky, which, to his surprise, was no longer dark. Leo felt perplexed at the idea of looking out at the world from his bedroom window and watching the sunrise, only to realize he had stayed up all night. It gave him a sense of well-being and satisfaction, a pride that he couldn't comprehend. Suddenly, his eyelids no longer felt heavy, and he felt as though he had been filled with unfathomable amounts of energy, energy no longer channeled toward what was kept inside of his mind, however may be slightly. The fact that it was no longer night made him feel less alone, and liberated, surrounded by life and people—things inaccessible during a time completely devoted to rest, a time in which no one dared to stir, except him.

Leo proceeded to climb down from the windowsill and onto the desk that was in front of it, yawning loudly in the process, clumsily steadying himself once reaching the floor, closing the window slowly. He looked around the dark room, searching for an answer as to what he had seen, or if it was even . . . real. He decided it wasn't, considering the fact that it didn't seem possible in the slightest. Despite the darkness of the room, which was slowly being eaten away at by the rising sun peeking through the window, the single light emitted by the small digital clock on his nightstand pulsated in the distance, its red-lined numbers caught while changing from 5:59 to six a.m. He slowly crawled back into bed and pulled the sheets over his head until his body was completely engulfed in the soft fabric that covered his bed. His mind was buzzing, and he laid there, unmoving, for what seemed like hours. Despite this, at some point he drifted into a deep, seemingly infinite sleep.

Leo awoke to the sound of hushed voices that he figured were coming from another floor, which he was only able to hear because of the constant, muted silence that was strewn through the air in every part of the house. His parents' monotonous voices were clearly disputing over a matter in which he probably should have no concern over, as usual. However, after being well-rested in a spiritually-awakening way in which he couldn't fully describe, Leo decided he would have a listen, just this once, even though he knew that this would be a waste of time, time that could potentially be spent doing other things. He shrugged those thoughts off and stealthily descended the first staircase, and then the second, being extremely careful as to not step on a creaky floorboard or show any signs of being near their presence, which he knew they wouldn't be particularly fond of. He leaned over the banister, close to the wall, near a long corridor in which he could not be seen from below.

Chester was sitting up with tense, perfect posture, a hand on both of his knees, while Mary sat across from him, her face contorted with worry, with unknown anxiety, clutching her shoulders. Leo tried his hardest to listen, despite still not being capable of hearing every word of their conversation, varying in volume—rising, crashing, falling. This frustrated him greatly, and it was as though the silence of the large house wanted to drown out their wispy, satin words.

With the very few words that Leo heard, he could tell that Mary's voice was quiet, a mere whisper, although it contained fractals of aggressive tones within her way of speaking, making it evident she was upset.

". . . doesn't deserve it . . . didn't do anything . . ."

Chester spoke back to her, a hole—emotionless, empty, nonexistent.

". . . this is the only way to get it to stop."

". . . no . . . won't let it happen."

"It has to . . . eventually. It's not going to stop unless you let it happen, Mary. Nothing's happening to him, so someone has to . . . do it a different way. It doesn't always work."

Leo's eyes widened as a wave of panic rushed throughout his body, chilling his spine and making the palms of his hands clammy. He swallowed hard out of fear and frustration. His face felt hot as his heart began to race faster and faster. He was certain they could hear it from where they were. Leo gripped the banister while he attempted to calm himself down. He looked down once more at them only to find that Mary was staring up directly at him, her usual seemingly infinite eyes turned to shallow pools of emptiness.

Leo backed up quickly in horror, bumping into the wall, startling himself before quickly running back upstairs, back to his room, shutting the door and plummeting to the floor on the other side of it as fast as he could. The words that he had heard them saying echoed throughout his mind, resonating with it, taunting it.

His whole brain was exploding. There were just . . . too

many things. All slight, measly forms of reasonable measures for a situation such as this were disregarded when Leo, with a sudden new chaotic energy, ran back downstairs. He slipped on a pair of boots, lazily tucking the laces into the top, and ran out the back door. He ran past the empty houses, which always seemed vacant and hollow despite having people inside of them, and past the glistening mineral-like pavement, emphasizing the heat that the early sun brought with its birth.

After walking through what felt like miles and miles of undergrowth and shrubbery, Leo finally reached the river; a sanctuary that would embrace him in his time of fear and frustration, an internal turmoil he felt that no one else other than himself could comprehend—no one. He proceeded to sit down in his usual spot, which was beside a rock that looked like it towered way high up above your head if you sat next to it, but was actually not that big at all. Leo appreciated that small detail about the rock, which is why he chose to sit there.

He closed his eyes and breathed deeply, trying to put all of his thoughts into perspective, or line them all out in front of him at least. They couldn't have been talking about him . . . could they? What had he done wrong? Nothing made sense. And Chester said something about how . . . it would happen a different way. Leo squinted his eyes shut tighter and shook his head in frustration. He allowed his own words to resonate within himself, to reassure him, allowing his body to meditate and relax entirely, crafting a home out of the silent yet echoic ambience of the outdoors.

A boisterous, loud voice shattered the blissful silence.

"Hey."

Leo jumped and quickly looked around in shock, only to lay his eyes upon Willie.

"Jesus Christ, you nearly scared me half to death," Leo said angrily, smacking his friend's leg from below as Willie proceeded to laugh. Willie sat next to him, jutting his feet out into the water, not bothering to remove his already-ruined sneakers, which were beginning to fall apart more and more every day.

"What are you doing here this early?" Leo asked him, attempting to maintain a tone that didn't sound in any way offended by his presence when all he wanted was to be alone. But perhaps this was good for him.

Willie looked into the clear noisy waters that engulfed his feet, unblinking. He shrugged.

"I don't know. I just . . . couldn't sleep, so, I mean . . . I thought to myself, 'Hey, might as well wake up early.' Y'know? It happens to me sometimes," he yawned.

Leo looked up at him. "Yeah. The same thing happened to me. It's probably just because of what happened, I guess. I can't stop thinking about it. But when I can, it's not for very long."

There was a brief intuitive silence between the two, the chilled morning breeze surrounding their woeful bodies. Everything seemed, on some level, different to Leo. Everything was . . . calm, unmoving. It felt as though his house held him captive, forcing him to see, to hear things he wouldn't witness anywhere else: a whole other world, a cage, a trap, a tripwire. Everything within the hollow echoic halls filled him with unfathomable amounts of loneliness and anger toward no one, but perhaps toward himself—for not leaving, for allowing himself to be a part of the only thing he had ever known: infinite . . . aloneness.

After the intense emotions he had felt the night before, he felt he suddenly had an altered connection to the reality outside of his own. He felt as though he was looking in, but after his feet mingled with the cold water and the breeze blew through his hair, he realized he was actually looking out—looking out from his home in a perfect world in a perfect moment. He was already there. In this moment, everything seemed silent. The roaring waters were muted by the peaceful white noise that occupied the entirety of his mind. He felt as though he had finally come to know what peace was: finding the ability to tell himself to stop, to never lose control, to breathe, to forget.

He was startled slightly as, with a roaring, quick motion, Willie lifted both of his feet out of the water, the droplets dripping along the dry bank, creating trails and patterns of darkened dirt.

"Willie."

"What?"

Leo's lips parted and then then closed again in hesitation. He looked down quickly and then back up at Willie before swallowing and continuing in his attempt to speak.

"L-let's go back," he stammered.

"Leo, why?" He said quickly, layers of fear unraveling in his shaky voice.

Leo's eyes went wide. The look within them screamed fear and desperation: extreme, agonizing, eternal desperation and curiosity that desired only to be quenched by what he desired, which was to return to the warehouse he had found. He sat up with a more tense posture, rising from the ground slightly.

"Please. I just have this . . . feeling. Like, I need to know more, even though it doesn't really matter. I just need something to distract myself from thinking about . . . her."

Leo's voice wavered a bit when he spoke. Willie sighed, and, with implied agreement, he stood up, looking up at Leo whose face lit up when he noticed that he was getting what he wanted.

"Come on, let's get this over with," Willie muttered, trailing behind Leo, following him out beyond the river, past everything familiar, and back into the moisture-laden air of lonely trail that led them deeper and deeper into the densely wooded forest. The path was nearly completely obscured, engulfed in an eerily familiar yet unfamiliar silence that hung in the air just days before.

CHAPTER SIXTEEN
The Return

Their footsteps up to the warehouse were certain, but their hearts told otherwise. Leo became nauseous as he knew they were drawing closer; he recognized the clearing, the dreary colors muted by the dry wind and melancholic trees with branches that hung down so low that their tendrils brushed lightly against the top of their heads occasionally. They both remained silent, the tense atmosphere choking their words away, forcing them to speak only in exchanged nervous glances, with shifty eyes and sweaty palms. The more Leo thought about what he was doing, the more he wanted to turn back. He clenched his jaw and tightened his fists, his fingernails digging into his hands. He felt angry at himself for giving in to his curiosity. With every step he took forward, the regret and fear that he contained festered up inside of his stomach swelled up so largely to the point where he had begun to shake, and his head no longer felt heavy, but light with panic. He was conscious of the fact that he was losing control slowly, but he knew he had to contain himself, for the sake of his sanity, for Willie.

Leo looked over to him and took notice of how his walking pace had seemed to quicken, but he couldn't tell if it actually was or not, because his thoughts felt as though they were lagging behind his body, and he wasn't present within his own physical form, but rather looking at himself from behind. Willie walked with a purpose, eyes set on only what lay in front of him, maintaining a straight, stern face that conveyed little emotion, an anomaly of mixed expressions that meant nothing.

The two pushed on without stopping once, without uttering even a single word. However, Willie seemed like he knew exactly how he was presenting his exterior; mysterious, enigmatic. The last thing he wanted was for Leo to know how he truly felt: desperate, fearful, yet curious. So curious, in fact, that he couldn't wait to reach the warehouse. With each step, with each minute that passed, he could feel all of the thoughts that were circulating throughout his head diminishing, shrinking, left in the dirt behind him, abandoned—for now. His heartbeat quickened when the clearing opened up further, the undergrowth subsiding, revealing the forgotten building. His shaking hands wiped his forehead of cold sweat and pushed strands of hair behind his ears, revealing his suddenly uncertain expression. He wanted this so badly, but now he wasn't entirely sure if it was worth it. However, the feeling of adventure and the potential thrill factor, which seemed inevitable, was too much for him to resist. He wanted nothing more than to take his mind off of Day and that whole horrible morning that seemed to last months. He swallowed hard and looked up; he and Willie were now directly in front of the building. Thunder rolled quietly in the distance, growling its warning in a low, foreshadowing tone. Leo didn't listen. He looked over to Willie, who had positioned himself right next to him, nervously digging into the dirt with his foot, creating a slight dent in the dry, barren soil.

Leo pushed the heavy door open, his heart pounding in his ears, all of the memories crawling back to him in a monsoon of fear, an intense yet desirable feeling that he found he couldn't resist any longer. He knew he had to carry on—not just because he wanted to, but because . . . he *needed* to. The more he thought about his seemingly sudden fixation on the place, the more he found it rather unusual, and the more he contemplated whether he even wanted to be here at all. He could only describe it as being . . . drawn to the building, sucked into its many mysteries, never to be understood by anyone. But the idea of it all was just irresistible to him—beautiful even. He couldn't stop himself from walking forward, an overwhelming desire for closure, distraction, and satisfaction coming over him, controlling his every move, causing him to walk deeper and deeper inside of the warehouse. His footsteps were made light and motivated, no longer weary and hesitant . Willie lagged behind him, desperate to keep up. Leo stopped abruptly, spinning on his heel.

"Come on."

"What's the rush?"

Silence.

Leo choked on his words. He didn't know what the rush was. He just . . . needed to be there, needed to be away from everything in his reality—in *their* reality. The dusty, humid smell filled his nostrils, fogging his brain. Leo sighed.

"I don't wanna be here right now."

Leo was silent for a few moments before answering.

"I'm sorry. I just really need this right now."

Willie rolled his eyes, continuing to walk but now at a much quicker pace than before.

They both walked up to the molded, narrow doorframe that led down into the familiar downstairs area, which reeked of decay , the rolls and stacks of fabric that lined the walls nearby emitting a muted smell similar to death. Leo looked at Willie, who was busy occupying himself by fiddling with some of the loose strings that hung down from the side of his shirt, pulling them out, and then watching them flutter to the ground.

"Are you ready?" Leo asked him in a slightly hushed voice.

Willie shrugged.

Together, they walked down the familiar winding staircase, strangely feeling as though they had descended down it many times, the fear they felt the first time in this place intricately etching the environment into their minds forever, never to be forgotten—thoroughly remembered. Leo glanced around. There was a small window that let in extremely minimal amounts of light, leaving the rest of the vast, open space shrouded in dark-ness, as the golden sunlight could only reach so far. The more they both took in the surroundings of the area, the less un-comfortable they felt. But, of course, they would never openly say to one another that they felt that way, and rather just kept it to themselves in fear of being thought of in a different way. Neither of them knew that the other wouldn't care. Leo broke the silence that hung in the dusty, molded air.

"I wanna look around. Let's split up."

Hesitantly, Willie agreed and allowed himself to wander away from his friend once they passed a narrow corridor, and Leo walked in the opposing direction while he found himself inside of the damp, dark office, which seemed much more abandoned and eroded than the last time they had been in it.

Willie glanced around the cramped, quiet office. The only audible sound to him was Leo roaming around in another room that seemed to be not too far away. He could hear his heavy footsteps stopping periodically, only to be followed by occasional rustling and rummaging. The light let in by the small window across from the room seemed to be much dimmer than he had remembered, and let off an eerie glow that faded slowly to black as he walked further and further inside of the cramped room.

In the adjacent room, Leo felt a chill slowly drift down his spine, a phantom tracing its invisible fingers over his bare back. He looked around slowly, peering into drawers, opening up cabinets, and hesitantly rummaging through severely damaged and molded folders and every single sodden old stack of paper that he could lay his shaking hands on. He found that most of the words printed onto the seemingly ancient papers were illegible, taunting him.

He reached his hand up until it reached the top of the filing cabinet, feeling along the top of it until he found yet another stack of papers. He pulled them down, and down with it came a small, worn, yellow notebook, which appeared to not have been moved for quite some time, as the majority of its weight was made up by the thick layer of dust that completely hid the front of the book entirely, making it appear way more dense than it actually was. He quickly brushed the immense amount of dust off, as his nose had begun to run and his eyes started to feel itchy. He cracked it open to a random page, squinting, struggling to read the small, spidery handwriting that made up the dated paragraphs within, which appeared to be journal entries.

January 8th, 1930
My dear nephew has come to visit me. Today will bring much excitement here in our humble family establishment. Everyone is seldom all in one place, especially since the holidays have just passed. It gets lonely, shipping out all this fabric, handling it day after day, doing absolutely nothing else. It gives no purpose to an already empty existence. But Daniel is filled with so much life—or at least he used to be. I grieve for the boy, as much as I do for my own losses. We, however, share the same loss. My sister—his mother—was taken from us in an accident,

not too far from here, in fact. He was such a lively boy. He doesn't say much anymore . Rather than vaguely talking, he'll sit by the window and watch the wind toss the curtains about. Poor Daniel. I'll look after him.

Leo furrowed his brow, reading the paragraph over and over, trying to make sense of it all, trying to understand if it even meant anything. He didn't even understand the phrase "mean anything" anymore, as there was nothing it could possibly even be related to, because he knew nothing of this place or of the people that he assumed were part of his family, which once worked tirelessly inside of the ginormous building that he now stood inside of. With shaking, sweaty hands, he closed the small journal with such a force that dust particles were disturbed, dispersing in all directions around him. He walked over to the front of the office, allowing the light to hit the small book, exaggerating its decay. He wiped yet another layer of dust from the front only to reveal small letters etched into the top-left corner. Barely legible, it read: "Floyd."

He could still hear Willie exploring the other rooms, and it seemed as though he was refusing to acknowledge him. Leo assumed that perhaps this was good, and was a sign of his recovery, one of which involved only himself and no one else. He allowed himself to sit down against the wall beside the filing cabinet, continuing to grasp the book in both hands. He felt rather invasive reading someone's journal, but since he was most likely related to these people in some way, since they shared the same last name, he felt slightly more at ease being in possession of such a personal item. He got comfortable and decided to continue reading where he had left off.

January 9th, 1930
Daniel's father has decided to allow him to spend the night here. It is very late now, and Daniel is so charming when he sleeps, so . . . peaceful—something that I envy with every inch of my heart. I cannot have this. I cannot have this peace, and it is driving me insane. Ever since that night that Alois tried to . . . drown me, I have this itch. An itch that cannot be satisfied, a constant nagging thought that I should . . . get rid of him. I also want to get rid of . . . everyone that has anything to

do with him. *I know these thoughts are impure. I don't know why I feel this way; all I know is that I must. I must. I must. I must. I must. I must.*

Leo was shaking, his immense fear beginning to overwhelm him so severely that he felt as though he could barely breathe. He knew he needed to keep reading, however, he was unsure of why. All he knew was that he needed to keep turning the pages and continue to let his eyes read over the same words countless times, allowing them to make less sense to him than they did initially.

January 15th, 1930
As we are still feeling the full force of winter's wrath here in our small, humble town, I have kept the fire lit all day. As Daniel's father won't be back for quite some time, I've decided to try and calm Daniel's nerves with some herbal tea. I've observed that he doesn't seem to like it, or rather, he doesn't like what I've done to it. The effects have yet to show. He just keeps staring down into the cup after every sip he takes and then looks up at me, as if he knows what I've done. He stares calmly up at me with those bulbous, brown eyes of his. He looks so wise, so distant. What have I done, what have I done? Oh, God, what have I done?

Leo gasped quietly to himself upon noticing that the closer to the end the writing got, the more illegible and rushed it appeared, the slanted, neat letters turning into barely decipherable symbols, mere disconnected lines. Still, he continued to read.

January 16th, 1930
It's too late. I've done it. What of Daniel? Daniel is . . . gone. And it's all my fault. Words cannot express the unfathomable amount of guilt I am experiencing. I can no longer function. My guilt, my shame, my impurities are all I think about anymore. I can't live. I can't live unless I continue to satisfy my desires. I can't stop now, and I have no desire to. Alois is next. And I'm not stopping there. Everyone—everyone—related to him will feel my extreme wrath, and I care little of the consequence that will arise from this, as no one is aware of my true capabilities. I have

spent years studying every single aspect of alchemy that I can—I know how to make people do what I want them to. Alois Acheron—and his bloodline—will be under my control, forever. And as for others that exist alongside me in this humble community of Thornbrook—I can make any of them do whatever I desire. They will listen to me! They will beg to be set free, but I'll never let them—never. I'll kill them if that's what they want. Thornbrook will be perfect—my tiny little magnum opus.

January 16th, 1930
With every person I take control of, the more elated I feel. Could this be what I was missing? I'm certain it is. Everything is perfect. I no longer feel guilt. I no longer . . . feel. This is good.

April 9th, 1954
I am beginning to take notice of what all of this immense power is doing to me. I am no longer aging. Since the demise of Alois, I couldn't feel happier. Everything is going so well. Despite believing for so many years that I had permanently lost the ability to process emotion, to this day I continue to experience an emotion continuously that only be described as guilt. Of course, the intensity of this emotion varies a lot. However, I have no control of when it begins to spiral out of control. Take now, for instance. It's doing it again. It starts as a slow, aching feeling that works its way up my body, starting at my feet. Then, a tiny, whispering voice begins to surface within my head. It speaks softly to me, then begins to yell, so loudly that it is almost completely unbearable, and I feel as though I want to peel back the layers of skin on my face and crawl out of myself, leaving the apparition behind with my physical being. Then, I begin having involuntary thoughts, such as the ones I am thinking now. I cannot put them into words, as they sound like many shrieking voices compiled into one, yet the one voice is overlapping itself, shouting many, many, many things at me, things that I do not understand. I want it out of my head. But, at the same time, it's nice to be me. I've built a new life in Thornbrook, all in my favor, all to myself. Is this wrong? God knows I'm miserable now, and there's a spot in hell saved for me, I know it, I just know it. My damnation is inevitable, but it is too late. I must carry out what everything—everyone inside my head is telling me to do.

Leo couldn't read anymore. He slammed the journal shut and threw it across the dusty wooden floor. It hit the side of the desk loudly, shaking it, causing it to knock down several items atop it, which all came crashing down loudly, shattering the morbid, dreary silence. He heard Willie's voice call out to him from quite a distance away.

"Are you okay in there?"

His voice was coated with an obvious startled tone that made it curve up in pitch.

"Y-yes," Leo answered, his voice wavering. The levels of anxiety he was experiencing made him feel like he wasn't even in his body, but rather looking down at himself from somewhere else. His head felt like it was going to burst open, his heart pounding so hard in his ears that it felt as though the sensation was vibrating his entire skull. He shakily climbed to his feet, suddenly finding himself struggling to breathe. All he wanted was to leave this place. Giving the journal one last look from across the small office room, he walked out through the doorframe and turned a corner in the corridor to find Willie. He wasn't going to tell him about anything that he had just read—for Willie's sake, and for his own. Just thinking about the jarring, manic words sent intense tingly feelings all over his body, rushing him with chills and a dizziness that he couldn't get to go away. He decided he would just push everything he had read to the back of his mind for later, among other things, which resided there also, such as Day, and various other occurrences that he wasn't too fond of thinking about.

He spotted Willie across the vast open area, who was squatted down in front of a chest of some sort, rummaging through its contents, in a way that made it appear as though he had known exactly what he was looking for before he even arrived. The amount of desperation in his movements was rather shocking to Leo, but decided not to say anything, as the amount of aggression he was noticing in his friend in recent days signaled to him that he was still in a rather sensitive state and desired no further provocation.

"Woah," Willie breathed, jogging over to Leo, who stood tensely, leaning up against one of the five cement pillars that seemed to support and assist in the framework of the old building. He looked up.

"Check this out."

Willie handed him a small piece of paper with skinny-lettered cursive handwriting on it, whose words leaned a little too far to the left. Leo took it from him, observing it, squinting at the tiny letters. It appeared to be a briefly-worded note of some sort. The handwriting was nearly illegible, and after reading from the journal he had found, he had very little interest in reading anything else from this place, terrified of what it would say. However, the excitement in Willie's eyes caused him to melt, and he didn't want to disappoint him, especially not now—not when he needed him the most. He sighed, and tried his best to read the words, barely managing to do it, yet he was extremely successful in the end.

June 2nd, 1975
Floyd,
We regret to inform you that after many, many years, we've obtained another deviant. This one is resisting treatment, but we're sure she'll give in soon. She has to. We know you've decided to stop killing the ones who don't respond to the first method of treatment, so we've developed an alternative that gives their bodies a second chance. Your wishes will not be taken lightly. We all hope that we will all be rewarded for our extreme level of adeptness. After all this time, things are finally coming together. Oh, Floyd, isn't this just what you wanted?
—W. Kaylock

Leo's eyes went wide as he read the letter once more. He read it over and over, until the slender, slanted letters began to blur together into nothingness. He felt the slow, creeping anxiety take on a new form, a being that attached itself to his back and didn't let go. His fears were the talons that dug deep into his spine, into his entire being. His heart raced. He swallowed hard, his mouth dry. He felt faint, and extremely dizzy. He could no longer hear anything other than his heartbeat and his labored breathing, his lungs feeling as though they were going to burst open. He couldn't stop thinking the same thoughts over and over and over again.

June 2, 1975, was . . . yesterday.

He couldn't understand how that would be possible, or what anything in this letter meant; it made absolutely no sense at all. His lack of understanding was so immense that he felt extreme anger and frustration towards the words, towards the writing, towards . . . Floyd.

Everything felt surreal. Life was redundant in this moment. In this building, he was no longer himself, but rather a being that was living dead, a being whose only purpose in this world was to search, and search, and read, and panic. All for what? Nothing. Nothing would come of it, and it meant nothing to him. But the frustrating part was that, on some level, it meant the entire world to him, and he was drawn to the idea of finding out more about these things, and the more he told himself he didn't care, the less he believed it, and it made him just want to be here more and more.

However, he decided that this did not mean that he would tell him what he knew about "Floyd," about the journal he had found, or about the obscure date on the note he had handed him, which he'd seemed to overlook, as he hadn't mentioned anything to Leo about the oddity of it.

Leo looked up, only to be met with Willie's agitated expression. He assumed he had taken much longer to read it than Willie had assumed he would. It was shocking to him to see Willie that angered over such a miniscule thing.

"Sorry," Leo murmured, gently handing the letter back to Willie. Willie snatched it from him, ripped it up, and allowed the snowflakes for remains to descend to the ground slowly, twirling through the dank, stuffy air. Leo looked up at him in shock of his spontaneously destructive action. As though becoming suddenly conscious of Leo's immense surprise, he sighed and began to quickly explain himself.

"I-I just don't understand any of this. It's stupid. I just . . . want things to make sense. I can never get what I want. Why are we even here?" The desperation and angry tones in his wavering, stammering speech were becoming more apparent compared to earlier. He threw a large stack of papers down off of a nearby bookshelf. "This is stupid," he snapped as he aggressively tossed the fallen papers around. "All of it," he continued, as he stopped suddenly, breathless, standing in the middle of the hurricane as the rubble settled and everything was still once more. Leo could tell he was grieving, and he wasn't sure

105

how to help him, which was something he was beginning to find extremely frustrating, ever since the first day that Willie's odd behavior became noticeable. It hurt him to not see him happy, to not see him as the once careless, free spirit he once knew. He figured that with time, he would come back, and hoped that with all his heart. He wanted his best friend back, to help him through his adversities. They were both broken, and he knew two broken people trying to help each other mend was a lost cause. So, he would wait. And wait. And wait some more—as long as he needed to.

A rather brief silence passed before Leo spoke up. The air of the downstairs area of the warehouse seemed to be made up exclusively of dust, and he was beginning to feel as though he was choking, suffocating even. He looked around one last time before speaking.

"Come on. Are you ready to get outta here?"

Willie nodded, his gaze already directed towards the narrow staircase that led back up into the main area of the building, the staircase that carried them further away from hell, and closer to freedom.

The two headed back upstairs in silence, the sound of the narrow creaking staircase muted by their nerves, their racing thoughts that compelled them to continue walking. The duo suddenly stopped short when they heard a creak behind them. Willie peered at Leo through the dusty black of the room.

"Was that you?" he asked his friend, hoping with all of his heart that he would say yes.

". . . No," Leo answered him, looking around.

They decided to ignore it and proceeded to walk up the stairs again. This time, they heard heavy footsteps, right on their heels. Willie whipped around, only to be met with a cloaked figure sporting a plain blue velvet mask, holes revealing only his eyes.

Willie, frozen in terror, wanted to choke out a dry scream, but he didn't dare make a sound. Practically jumping over Leo, he dashed up the stairs and out of the building as fast as his long legs could carry him. Leo was right on his heels, his heart pounding, his temples feeling as though they were about to explode. They ran through the undergrowth behind the building, not daring to look back into the foggy, dark-green abyss.

CHAPTER SEVENTEEN

A Struggle

When they felt that they were far away enough, they rested their heads against a gentle sloping rock, both panting and exhausted.

"See . . . Willie . . . I . . . told you . . . I saw it before," Leo said between swift, shallow breaths.

Willie didn't say a word. His eyes were wide, his entire body shaking. He was paralyzed in fear. He tried to speak, tried to part his lips, but it was no use. His knees felt weak. His muscles, his bones felt fragile and weary. He couldn't stop shaking. Pushing his long hair from out of his eyes, he shook his head slowly.

"That . . . that wasn't . . . real. It couldn't have been."

Despite his words, Leo could tell from Willie's disquieted expression that in his heart, he knew it was very, very much real. Everything was, and it was as clear and vivid as day. Day. Day. Day was gone. Leo still didn't want to believe it was true. When he woke up, he hoped that everything was just a nightmare, well thought-out illusion of his mind that meant nothing. But no. He was here. Day really was gone, and everything was real.

Leo could tell that Willie was doing everything in his power to prevent himself from fainting, fading away, collapsing. He could tell that he couldn't hear anything Leo was saying to him, his words mere smudges across an already overly-crowded canvas, the colors in his words inaudible, invisible. He knew the way back, and that was all he decided to focus on, and that was all he felt he *needed* to focus on: one foot in front of the other, as fast as he could. He treaded faster and faster, until he could no longer see Willie behind him. All he could hear was the crunching of leaves beneath his feet, and the brisk night air sliding past his ears, rustling his hair.

You deserve this, he thought to himself, furrowing his brow as a lump swelled up in his throat as he began to hold back the tears that were blurring his vision. As he found that he was nearing closer to familiar surroundings that didn't make him feel curious or uncomfortable, he had begun to feel calm, happy even, but more like a numbness that took over his mind that he mistook for happiness. Either way, he was much more fond of this feeling, rather than running through the woodland landscape in a blind panic, desperate to get away from everything.

He looked over his shoulder worriedly, suddenly feeling an immense amount of guilt for leaving Willie by himself. He began to panic. What if he wasn't even following him? What if he got lost? A million thoughts suddenly made their way through his hollowed head, none of them reassuring. His heart began to race again as he turned back around and started to retrace his steps. The air smelled damp and dewy. He looked up at the swollen sky. The clouds appeared to be right above his head, whispering to him, threatening him with pinprick-like drops of water poking his body, soon to turn into fat droplets that threw punches. Sure enough, in a seemingly abrupt maelstrom of sound, a storm was initiated, the roaring thunder rattling his insides, shaking the earth.

"Willie!" he called out into the growingly frigid air, which was further chilled by the intense downpour that grew harsher and harsher by the minute.

He continued to walk deeper into the forest, back onto the barely noticeable path.

"Willie!"

There was no response. His head spun as he felt his panic returning, biting him all over, his chest unable to move up and down quick enough for his shallow breaths.

Suddenly, he felt a hand being gently placed on his shoulder. He whipped around, gasping slightly, and looked up. It was Willie.

"Are you okay?" Willie asked him. "I was right here the whole time. Why were you calling for me?"

Leo looked past him in immense confusion.

"N-no you weren't," he stammered, his lip quivering.

Willie shrugged before responding.

"Well . . . I was. Come on, let's keep going. It's freezing."

Calmed by Willie's voice, Leo complied, and hung back behind him, letting him lead the way back. Willie gripped all of his hair into one hand, and squeezed the water from it, only to have it weighed down by the rain again. Neither of them spoke a single word, even when they made it to the end of the forest, and back into civilization, familiarity. They then followed a sidewalk, which carried them back to another clearing that allowed them to make the all-too-familiar walk back to their safe cradle of a neighborhood.

Upon reaching the water-drenched neighborhood, Leo only had one thing in mind, and he knew he didn't have to say a word. How could he, anyway? He didn't want Willie to see that he was on the verge of tears, and he thought about how choked his voice would sound if he attempted to speak. As soon as they neared close enough to his house, Willie took off running through the slanted rain, through the mist, disappearing entirely. He ran up the stairs that led to the porch of his house, took one last look out at the blurred world, and slammed the door—hard.

Leo was left alone, standing in the middle of the large cul-de-sac, the rain coming down in sheets all around him, covering his body in chills, filling his eyes with water, and dusting his eyelashes with small constellations. He surprised himself, as somehow, he wasn't confused as to why Willie would run. His brain was clouded by the rain, and if he was honest with himself, he would've found that he didn't really care why his friend ran. All he knew was that he was happy that they were home safe and no longer roaming around at that stupid warehouse doing virtually nothing productive. However, since no distractions were left, he found himself thinking, thinking way too hard about all of the things he had told himself to save for later; Day laying lifelessly before vanishing into nothingness, never to be seen again, the glowing apparition of a woman that reached her hand through the middle of his body, the masked figures lurking in the shadows, the letters and journal entries written in that foreboding spidery handwriting.

No, not now, he thought to himself, growing frustrated as all of his thoughts began to escape from where he had hidden them away. He shook his head angrily as he began to quicken his pace significantly, running as fast as he could towards his house, which was only a short distance away from where he was standing. *No, no, no, no*, he thought as his head pulsed, providing him with countless images, countless vivid images of everything he didn't want to see ever again. There was no controlling it. There was no stopping it. It was too late—far too late.

He quickly climbed the steps to his house, stumbling a bit. Not bothering to close the front door, he ran to his room, and allowed himself to collapse slowly up against the wall. Breathing quickly, he closed his eyes tight, raising his shaking fingers to his temples, attempting to soothe the headache that was arriving, growing in intensity the more anxious he felt. He thought about the woman he had seen. Dream or not, it seemed real—very real. As much as he would have liked to deny her being real, he knew it was true, and there was nothing he could do about it. Images of Day flashed through his mind, both alive and . . . dead. Some of the images weren't even real, yet some of them were. He couldn't tell the difference anymore.

Worst and most vivid of all, he couldn't stop thinking about what he had read in that journal. It made so little sense, yet so much sense. Even if it concerned people that had no part in his life whatsoever, he had a strong feeling of fear and responsibility directed towards what he had read—every part of it. Every word was a scream, the building a song made up of chaotic noise that lured him in, beckoning him to walk closer and closer until he was trapped, forced to listen to every single shrieking note within the melody of madness. The words he had read played over and over again in his mind, begging him, pleading him to understand more, to uncover more about . . . whoever those people were.

The harder he forced his eyes shut, the more vividly he could picture the lurking man in the mask that they had run from, and he could still see Willie's look of disbelief as he tried to explain to him what he had seen. But now he found he felt less isolated in his sightings, knowing that, finally, Willie had seen it too.

One thought led to another, and suddenly Leo found himself beginning to think about the woman again. Chills rushed down his spine, as he could still picture her reaching out to him, her weak, shaking arms a cry for help, a warning—a threat.

Her featureless face closed in on his, and if he concentrated hard enough, he could still see her drawing closer and closer until she reached into him, which was when he had begun to feel that . . . coldness, a chill of such immense intensity that it was indescribable. It filled him with confusion, and just thinking about how it felt left him feeling rather disoriented.

Lifting his head up, he glanced over to his bed, memories of that night rushing back to him. The sleepless, stirring mental torture he had experienced that night was something he would never forget, although he was certain that, with time, he would think less of it. But now was certainly too soon, because just being in his room made him feel extremely uneasy. He glanced across from himself at the door, which was opened slightly, and closed it, afraid to see the same nearly shapeless figure lurking in the empty halls. He refused to see her again, and he decided to do everything in his power to make sure that that would be true.

The house was completely silent, the only sound present being the rain hitting the roof aggressively, begging to be let in. Leo listened to it intently, jumping a little when thunder sounded not too far away, rattling the windows. He wondered how Willie was doing. He wondered about a lot of things in that short span of time.

The majestic sounds of rolling thunder had begun to travel away, but the lightning, a strobe, lit up the dark room periodically, filling it with blinding white light. Shakily, he climbed to his feet and walked to the nightstand by his bed to turn the lamp on, which filled the room with a reassuring golden glow. He then walked over to his closet and quickly closed both of the doors, making sure that he couldn't see into the slight opening in the middle. Looking around the room one last time, he climbed into bed and allowed himself to close his eyes. He had decided that tonight would be the night that he would sleep, and he would enjoy it. He realized that he had gone to bed earlier than usual. However, he was still eager to be met with the dark paradise of sleep, which was something he had been a stranger to for quite a while lately. He took immense satisfaction in the idea that the idea of sleep was another plane of existence in which he was unaware and only he existed. Despite not being conscious of the fact that only he existed in this dimension, he just knew that he was the only one there, and he delighted in that fact. He loved the euphoric feeling of being on the verge of sleep, or staggering in between consciousness and unconsciousness. The way he was forced to give in to his mind and forced to allow it to make him think of anything or imagine anything involuntarily. Although he had no control in this state, and not all of the things he saw in his head were good things, he liked how it made his body at peace, floating towards nowhere, within nothing.

However, that night, his mind wouldn't let him reach his surreal dream state, the nirvana he had created for himself with only good thoughts and no intrusions. He clenched his eyes shut, hoping to sleep, hoping to stop thinking. In this moment, there was nothing he wanted more than for his mind to stop talking to him, to stop repeating itself—to disappear. His whole body felt extremely tense, even after he tried to relax it, concentrating first on his shoulders, letting them drop down slowly, then his fists, his back, and then his legs. This left him feeling shaky and restless. He opened his eyes and allowed his thoughts to be liberated, as he was exhausted of keeping them inside of their cages, held together by neurotic paranoia and fear of them escaping. His heart was beating harder and harder as sweat began to encase his entire body. A constant, dull ringing filled his head, muted by the sound of his heartbeat screaming into his ears. All he could think about was the warehouse, and Day, and all of the strange things he had found. It ate at him; he was itching for answers. He couldn't concentrate. Eventually, the realm of sleep claimed him, and he started to dream.

At first, everything was black. There was no noise. He was sitting in a chair that felt to be high up. The dead silence engulfed him tightly, like a blanket. After a while, the only noise that surfaced was the ringing in his ears that became more and more intense, seemingly amplified by the lack of noise. After a while, he heard many voices in the distance, talking in low, monotonous speech, almost chant-like. He tried to get up, but he couldn't; his wrists were strapped tightly to the arms of the chair. Every time he moved, the restraints felt tighter. It was painful. His eyes watered as the cold metal surrounding his wrists cut deep into his skin, deeper and deeper. It was unbear-able. No matter how much he wiggled and writhed, there was no escaping this. He sat there, agitated and panicked, waiting, preparing for the worst. He felt the fear crawl up his spine as he heard heavy, brisk footsteps drawing near to him. He braced himself, awaiting death—or worse.

Unexpectedly, the footsteps stopped. Leo was thankful he couldn't see; he didn't want to see what was about to happen. He could feel the presence of someone in front of him. He tried to calm himself by taking long, forced breaths. As soon as he began this, his face was met with the warm touch of anoth-er person's hand. It ran its fingers through his shaggy, ruffled hair, stroking the side of his face gently. The room was quiet. Leo was afraid. *What's happening?* he thought, his mind buzzing with the millions of questions he had, bouncing back and forth and echoing around inside of his skull.

Leo heard a brief clinking of what sounded like metal, but it was high-pitched, like a small silver bell. The footsteps walking towards him resumed. He blinked, and suddenly he could see again, the fluorescent light in what seemed to be an operating theatre blinding him as the silhouette of a person who appeared to be a woman—the same woman from before—lingered in front of him, saying nothing. He felt the same familiar coldness creep over his body as she neared closer to him. She held an elongat-ed needle filled with a phlegm-like, creamy black liquid. Some of it squirted out and fell to the floor, making a fizzing noise.

The masked woman looked at him reluctantly as she came toward him with the needle. Leo knew what was going to hap-pen. He tried to speak, tried to protest, but nothing would come out. He could no longer hear anything, his anxiety creat-ing a barrier of static that left out reality and he couldn't hear over. The cloaked figure grabbed him by the neck, injecting the liquid into him. His body tingled for a brief moment be-fore falling completely numb. He couldn't move. He couldn't feel anything, except for a sense that he was drowning as the black, foaming liquid began secreting from his mouth. He be-gan choking.

Leo awoke with a start, his entire body drenched in sweat, his wet hair stuck to the sides of his face. His whole body was shaking as he climbed out of bed. He threw on his yellow jacket, not bothering to change out of what he had slept in. He shoved his hands deep into his coat pockets and groaned. He was so caught up in reading through the journal he had found that he had forgotten about the new documents he obtained during his last visit to the dreaded warehouse, which he felt he was addicted to visiting, finding that he was somehow subconsciously addicted to uncovering more information, more secrets. He hoped one day that it would all end. He hoped that one day, he wouldn't have to think about any of this anymore.

Out of the folded, soggy stack of papers, he pulled out yet another letter. This one had a faint, faded address printed neatly on the old envelope, yellowed and molded with age. The narrow, handwritten letters looked perfect, like they could have been typed. The address read: *2966 Sky Circle*. Leo didn't bother to open the envelope; he was convinced nothing it said would help him at this point—he was just going to have to see for himself, which meant going to this address. He knew this street name; however, he had never once been down the narrow, winding paved street that opened up into another cul-de-sac, seemingly identical to Leo's neighborhood. Leo didn't know why, but he felt an extreme need to go there—*now*. He was reluctant to consider the idea of going alone, the feeling of hollow yet heavy loneliness and fear at the pit of his stomach growing, blossoming into adrenaline. But still, he told himself no. He wanted to take Willie, his only remaining friend. Even though Leo felt remorse for putting him through such a scare during the times he dragged him along on trips to the warehouse, he felt as if Willie was a part of this too—even though, deep down, he knew it was only him.

As he walked to Willie's, the rainy weather and swollen clouds up above made the air outside feel thick, like suffocating in heaps and heaps of cotton. The air smelled of dirt, which seemed to be intensified by the humidity. Frantically, Leo knocked three times quickly on his friend's quaint wooden front door before being met with Willie's gaze through the small window in the door. Willie turned the doorknob slowly, peering at him through the door he had opened ajar. He looked sickly and pale, his usual lively, dancing green eyes glazed over, tainted with lack of sleep. He appeared rather annoyed. Leo looked down to the ground, shifting his weight, making the fractals of rocks beneath him crunch loudly. He scratched the back of his head and looked up again. "Hey, um, so I found this envelope w—"

"No," Willie said, stopping him. He tiredly looked off into the distance, sighing, massaging his temples. Leo looked at him, shocked. He felt as though *he* was the one who was dragged into all of this, not Willie. He opened his mouth to argue, but then proceeded to shut it immediately, as Willie was beginning to speak again.

"Leo, I-I can't keep doing this."

His voice was hoarse and raspy—lifeless, sick.

"It doesn't feel right. It's something we probably shouldn't even know about. And it's . . . ruining me. It's ruining *us*. It's . . . all I can think about anymore, and I really want that to stop. I'm sorry," he said, before closing the heavy door back gently. All that remained was Leo's reflection shown in the glass window centered in the door, staring back at him.

As soon as Willie closed the door back, he drifted back over to the armchair in the parlor, which was where he had been sitting since last night. He hadn't slept, and he was finding that he was beginning to feel the effects of such a poorly made decision. His eyelids felt heavy, and if he didn't blink enough, they would close slowly on their own, causing his head to fall forward before he caught himself, and blinked and squinted his eyes several times in order to wake himself back up.

He got up slowly, walked heavy, tired footsteps into the kitchen, grabbed a glass from an already-opened cabinet above the stove, and filled it with water from the tap. He drank it slowly, the coldness of the liquid filling his insides with chilling tingles. He wrinkled his face in disgust and poured the rest of the water out into the sink. It tasted strongly of rust and lead. He set the glass down gently onto the counter and retreated back into the room he had just come from, sinking back into the chair, defeated. Since . . . that day, he didn't feel like doing much of anything anymore, and only mentally had enough energy to sit and do nothing except play around in his own head, his thoughts taking him down paths that he didn't really want to go down, but it left him no choice.

He sighed because he knew he could only blame himself. He was the one who told him about the warehouse. He couldn't figure out if he should be mad at him or appreciative of his selflessness. It had been a few days since the camping trip, and Willie had expected himself to be over it by now, or at least numbed significantly. But he still felt a strong sadness that grew from the core of his being, spreading and manifesting itself into everything he did, everything he touched, making him feel stuck—isolated even. Every day, he felt a hole in his heart, a hollow space that nothing could ever fill up again. He always felt on the verge of tears, accompanied by the lump in his throat that never seemed to want to go away. Devastation overtook every facet of his life, making even the simplest of actions impossible, purposeless.

He felt strange for feeling this way, as he had only known Day for a small amount of time that seemed like nothing and everything at the same time. With her brief existence in his life, he felt as though she provided something that Leo could not: a feeling. A warmth that could not be described. A longing, an intense longing to know her, to be part of her life, to be known by her on a deeper level than what he had with anyone else. It was different, and he didn't know why. Within those short days, he thought about her more than anything, more than anyone, more often than he breathed. Although he knew she was gone, the feeling was still there—stronger than before, blossoming, swelling in his chest, making him feel nauseous and tired.

His stomach churned with regret as he lay down onto the couch, closing his eyes. His muscles began to tense up, and he felt as though he was going to be sick. His hands began to shake with anxiety, his body growing weaker as he found himself once again caught up in the seemingly perpetual thought that he could have saved her, if only he had been more responsible. This thought, this singular thought, caused him to be at war with himself, one side of him believing it, the other knowing that he couldn't have saved her. This side, however, was always drowned out by the other. The other told him over and over how it was his fault, how he never should've let it happen, how everything would be perfect if they hadn't gone. He opened his eyes once more, his vision filled with hot, angry tears that stained his face with sparkling, starry streaks. *You're stupid*, he thought to himself. *Stupid.*

CHAPTER EIGHTEEN
Everything Was White

Day awoke in a numb stupor, lifting her body up from the bed. She winced as pain immediately shot through every inch of her body, quickly waking her from her daze. She looked down at her pale legs. It felt as if phantom knives were cutting into her legs at a rapid pace, refusing to give up until her legs became detached from her body. The sensation took her breath away, paralyzing her for a few seconds until it became slightly less intense and she could move again. She proceeded to massage her legs gently, although it did not have any effect on the pain, nor did it hurt to touch them. It felt . . . internal. Suddenly, the pain stopped altogether, leaving as quickly as she had woken up and realized it even existed in the first place. She breathed a sigh of relief, as she found she was finally able to concentrate on her senses.

She glanced around the room she was in and found herself entering a state of panic. The room was extremely small and contained nothing more than a bed and a large floor-length mirror. Everything was a bright white, except for the sheets that covered the mattress; those were a sickeningly old, off-white color, which reminded her of coffee-stained teeth. The room itself smelled of aged linen, the way an old house would. This, however, was not a house.

She walked around the small room, her eyes wide in panic, taking note of how small it was. The lack of windows didn't make her feel any better. She looked into the mirror, observing herself closely. Her thick, dark hair seemed longer, her already frail figure leaner. Or maybe it only appeared that way, as she found she was dressed in a rather oversized jumpsuit made from red material, contrasting greatly against the white walls. She looked past her reflection and gasped, noticing a door next to the foot of the bed. She walked over to it quickly, no longer desiring an explanation for why she was here or what this was, but suddenly consumed by the overwhelming desire to get out. The door was also painted white, and from what she could tell, had a window that was painted over, making it useless. She gripped the singular handle of the large metal door firmly and pulled as hard as she could. It was no use; the door was locked.

Suddenly, a burst of adrenaline and anger rushed through her, as she had begun to remember what had happened; the man—the doctor—looking down at her, his face the reflection in a funhouse mirror. She remembered a bright light, then darkness. She decided that she would not be kept here, and she would do whatever it took to get out, and never be anywhere near those people ever again, and definitely not be locked in this room again. She pulled, and pulled, and pulled. The white metal door groaned and shook, but it wouldn't budge; she knew it wouldn't, but she allowed herself to try one last time. Nothing.

She kicked the door in frustration before plopping back down onto the small bed to catch her breath. Tears filled her eyes as she allowed her body to sink down until she wasn't sitting up anymore, and instead just lying there. She stared up at the white, blank ceiling, trying to understand. Everything in her mind was cloudy, a dream, a distant memory. She felt the place of her wound, tracing her fingers along the slight scars that texturized her soft skin, repeating this action for what felt like hours, her eyelids slowly growing heavy. She longed to know what time it was, or what day it was at least. She allowed her eyes to close slowly, giving in to the temptation of no consciousness, an escape from a world she no longer understood or cared to understand, a world she only longed to disappear and slip away from. If only she could turn invisible and walk through the walls of the room. She could go back home . . .

Day's thoughts were interrupted with the sound of the lock of the door clicking open. Her body jumped slightly in shock, her heart racing faster and faster when she heard the door begin to open, the squeaking an unbearably high-pitched sound that scraped away at her eardrums. It slowly opened wider and wider before stopping, leaving the door only left open ajar. Her eyes widened in surprise as she listened harder and found that she could hear voices, small voices whispering to one another, only some words making their way through the slight crack between their world to hers, making themselves audible to her ears.

"What will we do with her?" she heard one say. "She's resisting treatment, and she has been for days now."

"We'll . . . keep trying," another responded. "It's going to work eventually. It has to."

The conversation trailed off into nothingness after that, and all three of the voices became completely silent. Day clenched her fists in frustration. She confirmed that they were in fact talking about her, when suddenly the door opened all the way, revealing a friendly woman holding a clipboard. She closed the door quickly as she sashayed deeper into the room. The far-away look in her twinkling eyes told Day she definitely wasn't genuine, but she decided to give her a chance. It didn't matter anyway. She had already decided that she was going to get out of here soon enough.

The woman came face-to-face with Day, smiling widely. She took a pen from out of her many pockets and clicked it so that the point came out. She was clad in strange attire that appeared to be some sort of work uniform. It fit her snugly, revealing her curves. She didn't seem to notice Day glaring at her angrily. She tapped her clipboard using the top of the pen, without taking her eyes off of Day.

"Hello," she said in a completely monotonous voice. "Could you please give me your name?"

". . . Day."

The woman nodded her head, still smiling, remaining unblinking. Once again, without taking her eyes off of Day, she scribbled her name down onto a piece of paper attached to the clipboard and then left, closing the door gently behind her. When Day heard the door click, she sighed in confusion. The way the woman never blinked and how she never stopped smiling sent chills down her spine, her nerves causing her body to shake, her muscles tensing, her thoughts racing. Suddenly, she no longer felt like she should escape. At least, not just yet. She found herself feeling extremely tired again and allowed herself to lay down, staring up at the obnoxiously low ceiling that made her feel even more compressed than she already was.

After what seemed like many hours, her eyes flickered open

slowly, revealing a rather stout man dressed in attire similar to that of the woman she had seen earlier. She scooted back quickly from him, panicking. The man's blank gaze burned into her retinas. He didn't say a word. The silence of the cold room hung over their heads, pressing down on them. The quiet, still energy that filled the room made Day feel even colder, more distant from reality.

The man raised a singular, pale finger, pointing in the direction of the heavy door, which was open. Day's heart raced, trying to see as much as she could beyond the door without turning her head or moving her body, careful not to exhibit any sign of interest. Emotionlessly and expressionless, the man gestured for her to leave. Day quickly scrambled to her feet, the bottoms of her bare feet hitting the cold, white floor hard. She stumbled out the door, eager to see what awaited beyond the metal heavy boundary, the only thing that stood between her and freedom.

She was wrong. As soon as she walked past the doorframe, she was met with several people with the same clothing as the man in her room. Some of them wore perpetual, empty smiles; others sported neutral but hollow expressions. They ushered her along, guiding her across a large, empty white corridor that opened into a room with many tables, each with people sitting at them, all wearing the same red jumpsuit that Day was dressed in.

The apparent staff members watched her from behind as she walked deeper into the large room. She found a table that no other people were sitting at and allowed herself to sink down into the cushioned chair slowly, glancing around nervously. The sound of many voices talking at once buzzed in her ears, feeding into her nervousness. But she decided that it was better than the absolute silence she had experienced in that small room with the bed.

Without warning, the room suddenly fell dead silent, and everyone's attention was directed toward a woman walking through a pair of double doors near the opposite end of the room, wheeling in a large cart with racks, each rack containing a different plate of food. From all sides of the room, the people in the red jumpsuits began springing up from their seats, eagerly gathering around the cart, each grabbing a plate of whatever they wanted, before hurriedly rushing back to their seats to eat. As they returned, the stagnating, loud noise of the room slowly returned, steadily growing louder and louder until it became the volume it was initially. It was in this moment that Day realized how insanely hungry she was. The amount of plates left on the racks was dwindling fast. Driven by her hunger, she got up and sprinted over to the cart, reaching down to the bottom shelf and grabbing the last one. She gasped as she felt someone else's hand brush up against hers slightly, causing her to pull her hand away from the shelf quickly.

"Take it," she heard a lively, deep voice say to her from above.

Day looked up, meeting the gaze of a very tall young man with spiky, bright red hair. He smiled at her, his large mouth spreading his grin wide across his face, his white teeth seeming to glow. Without taking her eyes off of him, she took the plate, slowly walking back to the table that she had been sitting at.

"Hey, come with me," he said to her, placing a heavy hand on her back, guiding her away from the direction she was walking in. Day complied, and allowed herself to be led away from an area that was unfamiliar and strange to another area that was unfamiliar and strange. The only difference was that the one she was being taken to had people, which she wasn't sure she was too fond of—especially not now, not here.

He led her to a table that many other people were seated at. The table was round, and once Day found an empty spot to sit next to him unfamiliar eyes stared into her soul from all directions, filling her with racing thoughts, drenching her in a cold, nervous sweat as she felt her face and the tips of her ears slowly turn red. She looked down and stared into her lap, her sweaty hands gripping the baggy jumpsuit that hung loosely against the upper part of her legs. The young man smiled widely, allowing the silence that came over the table once Day sat down to last a few moments longer. Before speaking, he glanced around at everyone at the table and cleared his throat.

"You guys, this is one of the new ones!" he exclaimed loudly, gesturing toward her before resting his arm on her shoulder. Everyone at the table looked up at her, suddenly intrigued, fascinated, infatuated with her. They all smiled at her, or at least gave her implied approving looks. As she looked at everyone in the circle, she realized each face was drastically different from the other, and everyone seemed to vary greatly in age: young, old, somewhere in between. When the young man with the red hair realized no one seemed like they were going to say anything, he began speaking again, filling the static of unheard conversations in the distance with noise of his own.

". . . So, I'm Joey," he began, gesturing toward himself. He gestured to the boy sitting next to him, who seemed to be around the same age as Joey. "That's Aiden, my twin."

Day was shocked; they looked nothing alike. Aiden was much paler and had long, platinum-blond hair that looked to be extremely damaged because of the vast amount of split ends coming from the ends of his short statement fringe, which barely even covered half of his forehead. He nodded slightly at her without making any sort of eye contact. Joey then pointed to the man that was seated next to Aiden, staring away into nothingness.

"That's Samuel." Samuel suddenly turned his head when he heard Joey say his name. "He doesn't say much. But he likes plants and stuff. The flowers in the front look amazing 'cause of him. Next to Samuel—that's Rowan."

Rowan was a small woman who appeared to be at least in her late forties. She had a small, frail body that contrasted greatly next to Samuel, who had a strong build, his dark skin accentuating every muscular bulge in his arms.

Day forced a slight smile, glancing around at everyone's faces. *How can they be so calm?* she thought. Strangely, their calmness made her feel even more anxious about being here, about being trapped here with no means of escape. She felt the onset of choking panic once more. She felt as though at any second, she would no longer be able to control her emotions and would break down and scream, or cry—or both. When the group seemed to have lost interest in her presence and went back to eating, she looked up at Joey, who was drumming his fingers lightly against the table, staring at Day's plate, a faraway, longing look in his eyes. He raised his eyebrows when he realized he had been caught.

"Are-Are you gonna eat that?" he asked hesitantly, looking down, smirking with guilt.

Day shook her head slowly. She no longer felt hungry at all.

Her appetite had been dwindled away, reduced to nothing after witnessing how sickeningly comfortable everyone seemed to be here, in this prison, in this white, barren cage. She continued to shake her head, over and over, growing angry as she began to think harder about the unbelievably confusing situation that she was in. She felt her eyes beginning to swell up with tears. She couldn't hold them back any longer and allowed just a few to escape from her eyes, leaving tracks in her soft, delicate face.

"Woah, are you okay?" Joey asked her between mouthfuls of bread.

Day shook her head.

"I need . . . to ask you something."

Joey shrugged his shoulders.

"Yeah, okay. Go ahead."

". . . Can we be alone?" she whispered, leaning in so he could hear.

Samuel caught notice and eyed both of them curiously.

Joey shrugged again.

"Um . . . alright."

He stood up, pushed his chair in, and walked away from the table, gesturing for Day to follow him. She walked with him down the same narrow corridor that she had entered the room from. This time, she followed him down another section of the hallway that led to a lobby area, the one part of the seemingly huge building that wasn't completely white. It was a cold, quiet room with many paintings on the walls, nice furniture, and potted plants guarding every corner, making the room appear drastically smaller than it actually was. Joey led her quickly through that room and slowly opened a set of wooden double doors, revealing a patio area. The blinding sunlight made Day's skin tingle, but in a good way, and caused her to squint and shield her eyes.

I'm . . . outside, she thought to herself. Many thoughts of her making a run for it in that very moment crossed her mind, but her hopes were all suddenly shattered at once when she looked out past the large outdoor area and noticed a large, thick wall, which seemed to be slightly higher than twenty feet, shielding them in, locking her, along with everyone else into . . . whatever this place was. Her heart sank, as she knew getting out was proving to be much harder than what she had thought, which was why she wanted to talk to Joey.

Joey allowed his body to sink down against the wall, sitting on the paved cement ground. Day sat next to him, situating herself as she listened to him speak.

"So, what did y'wanna ask me?"

Day hesitated.

"Do you . . . do you know why I'm—we're—here?" she stammered, looking up at him, waiting intently for an answer.

Joey's face grew serious as he gazed back at her. Day could feel her face tensing up and her worried eyes widening. Suddenly, Joey let out a huge laugh, causing Day's shoulders to relax a little. Joey grinned.

"No one knows why they're here!" he yelled, throwing his arms up, looking around as though he was expecting an audience that didn't exist to react to what he was saying.

Joey picked up on Day's confusion and leaned in, beginning to whisper to her.

"I really, honestly don't know why I'm here. All I can tell you is, one day, when I was . . . around twelve, I think, I just . . . woke up in a white room, in a bed. And all of the people that work here are like ˙. . . crazy or something! I don't know. They all just act . . . so weird. And they'll never talk to you directly, but sometimes I eavesdrop on them when they think none of us are around, and I hear things—strange things. Something about . . . treatments. They're trying to give us . . . treatments, to make us do . . . something. I don't know. Who cares! I don't mind it here," he said laughingly.

Her head was spinning with questions, and now, with answers. Nothing made sense. At least she didn't feel so . . . alone.

"How long have you . . . lived here?"

"Well, Aiden and I are twenty-three now, so . . ." He counted on his fingers. "Around eleven years."

Day's eyes widened in shock. She definitely did not want to be here for eleven years, or even eleven days, for that matter.

"And . . . and you never tried to leave? You're just okay with staying here, in a place you know nothing about? Don't you want to go back home?" She could feel her heart beating faster and faster the more she spoke.

Joey sat up, staring into her eyes, confused, and took a while before responding. He shrugged. "Nah. I'm okay here."

"Well . . . I need to leave," she responded, her voice wavering slightly.

Joey snorted.

"Good luck with that," he scoffed, slowly rising to his feet.

Day followed him back out into the lobby area and through the seemingly infinite hallways. She figured it was all up to her now, if Joey wasn't going to help her, which she knew he wasn't, because he simply didn't care. Day followed close behind him, careful not to get too close or too far away. The hallways were silent until Joey opened the double doors that led them back into the room with all of the round tables. The familiar noise flooded all around her, filling her with even more anxious feelings than she had when she was outside, alone with Joey.

She sat down next to him again, taking one last look at everyone sitting around the table. Samuel was still in the exact same position that he was in when they had left. He was a man of very few words, and occasionally looked up from his book to mumble something unheard to Rowan. Her weak-looking, frail figure made her appear even older than she was, shrinking her form entirely, shriveling her up, crippling her. She glanced away quickly when they took notice.

Suddenly, a loud noise sounded from above their heads. Unshaken by the deafeningly loud noise, everyone got up, and began shuffling out of the room, filing out through the narrow door and into the hallway. She glanced around for Joey, Samuel, anyone she recognized, but it was too late; they had already left. Struggling to make her way through the crowd, Day tried her best to peer through the broad shoulders and windows in between peoples' heads in the dense cluster of heat. The mass was so big, in fact, that it was several minutes before she made it back into the hallway. Everyone in front of her had begun to form a straight line in order to fit through the narrow hallways, and, together as one, turned a corner that led to a direction that was unfamiliar to her. She had not been in this direction yet. Hesitantly, she followed the crowd, shoving her way through the loud mass of people.

To her surprise, the hallway opened up into an area that she vaguely remembered from earlier. To the left of that area, there was a set of double doors, similar to the ones that led into the lunchroom-type area that they were just in. The group of people in the front of the crowd pushed the doors open quickly, stopping to continue to hold them open for everyone else that followed close and tightly behind them. They were thanked periodically, and responded to each person that expressed their gratitude before going back to talking amongst each other.

When Day finally made it past the set of double doors, she was shocked to find what seemed like endless corridors and sections of numbered rooms, all identical to the one she had woken up in. Suddenly, she spotted a mass of bright red hair in the distance: Joey. Next to him was Aiden, who locked eyes with her for a split second before looking away and not turning back around.

"Joey!" She yelled through the buzzing noise of the hallway. Several people turned and looked in her direction.

Joey took notice of her and gave a small wave before turning his head back around to face forward again. He slowed his pace slightly, which allowed Day to catch up with him. She swam through the densely packed crowd, shoving her way through what felt like miles and miles and miles of people. Finally, after what seemed like hours, she found she was walking right next to him.

"What's going on?" she asked him, her voice wavering in a fearful, panicked manner.

Joey narrowed his eyes at her in confusion, as though she was already supposed to know what he was about to tell her. He slowed his walking speed even further before coming to a complete stop to bend down and talk to her. Aiden waited silently behind him, running his fingers through his short bangs. Joey glanced around quickly, as though he didn't want others to hear him, even though he spoke rather loudly.

"It's time for treatment," he said matter-of-factly. "Go back to the room you came out of, and they'll come for you eventually."

Day's heart raced. Suddenly everything was blurry, and the constant sound of voices around her was reduced to slurred murmurs, mere sneaky footsteps compared to the high-pitched buzzing that rang inside of her head constantly, growing louder and louder the more she thought about what Joey had just said. She felt her face burning hot, her entire body beginning to tremble. She felt like floating slowly to the white marble floor and never getting up again. She was taken out of her nerve-induced haze when Joey nudged her gently on the shoulder with his hand.

"Hey, relax it doesn't even do anything. At least not for a while. It works on some people here, and after it does, we never even hear from them again. Maybe they get to leave? Plus, they say it takes years for that to happen. And I've been here for . . . quite a while, and hey, nothing changed about me. Tell 'er, Aiden."

Aiden looked away, shrugging and nodding his head slightly.

"Yeah, see? You're gonna be fine. Bye!"

With that, Joey took off running down the hall, disappearing into one of the rooms on the right. Aiden continued to walk beside Day before eventually hurrying along and drifting away in the opposite direction.

Day sighed, continuing to walk around mindlessly, wandering the plain white halls in all directions, exploring each and every identical section, getting herself more and more lost. She suddenly came to the realization that she had absolutely no idea which room she had come from, and that she had no way of knowing. Every room was exactly the same—the only thing differing from one room to the other being the numbers stamped neatly into the upper right-hand parts of the doors. The hallways, once filled with countless amounts of people, were beginning to thin out until she could almost see the entirety of the floor, and everything around her began to appear bigger and bigger, causing her to feel small.

She walked around until everyone except her had gone off and away into their designated room. She allowed herself to sink slowly to the floor with her back pressed up against the wall, staring down into her lap, fearful of what would happen to her next. Her stomach churned violently and suddenly everything had begun to feel hot—sickeningly hot. She felt sweat beginning to cover her body, leaving it feeling heavy and weak. With shaking, uncontrollable hands, she gathered all of her hair up and threw it over her shoulder, draping it all over to one side so that it wouldn't touch her neck. She then proceeded to roll up the sleeves of the strange, red jumpsuit, instantly sighing in relief when cold air rushed onto the upper parts of her sweaty arms, rushing her with a refreshing feeling.

When she rolled up the sleeve that covered her left arm, she noticed a thin, plastic bracelet wrapped tightly over her wrist. She turned her hand over, taking notice of a number printed in a small, compact font on the opposite side of the white bracelet: 5288.

Day glanced around at the rooms, at the numbers that appeared on them. She figured that this number would correspond to the number on the room that was supposed to belong to her. She walked over to the nearest room: 4599. *How big is this place?* she thought as she continued to walk down the seemingly never-ending hallway, watching as the numbers increased in size: 4600, 4601, 4602.

She walked and walked, quickening her pace the closer she got to the corridor that led to an entirely different section of rooms, whose numbers were now in the 5000s. Her heart beat harder in her chest the closer she got to 5288. After what felt like many excruciatingly tense and boring millennia, Day looked up and found that she was directly in front of the room. Not just any room—*her* room. Sure enough, the door was unlocked, and when she stepped inside, the room was completely empty.

Hesitantly, she stepped further and further inside, the perpetual sense of impending doom she constantly found herself possessing beginning to swell up greatly inside of her chest. She closed the door slowly behind her, glancing around curiously and quickly at every corner of the room, immunizing herself from any potential threats or surprises. She sat down in front of the mirror, the cold floor no longer stinging her bare feet, which were now safely folded away underneath her calves. She gazed into her eyes through the mirror, observing everything about herself, looking for changes, for evidence that anything had happened at all. She felt she looked . . . smaller, weaker—lifeless. She pushed a few stray strands of hair behind her ears in order to get a clearer view of her shrunken face before suddenly deeming all of her paranoiac thoughts insignificant when a new one suddenly surfaced, making all of the other thoughts that drifted around inside of her head miniscule, pointless—purposeless.

Quickly, she unbuttoned a few of the top buttons of her jumpsuit to look at her chest, the place she knew she had been . . . stabbed. Then again, she wasn't quite sure if she had been stabbed or not. All she knew was that something had happened there; she could feel it. She traced her fingers over it and gasped as suddenly she began to feel an intense tingling sensation that began in her fingers and started to spread all throughout her body. This feeling then turned into a numbness, an all-too-familiar numbness that didn't spread, but rather came on all at once to every part of her body. With the last bit of strength she felt she had left, she quickly pulled her hand away from the area of her chest where she knew a scar had once been. Almost instantly, the numbness went away and was replaced with a brief, throbbing pain near the area where the wound had once been. Before she could react, the pain subsided.

Suddenly, Day felt an intense pain in her head, not quite like a headache, nor any other type of pain she had ever experienced. She clenched her eyes shut tightly, wincing. As the last wave of pain drifted slowly through her head, she gasped, as she could suddenly . . . see something. She realized she was . . . involuntarily remembering things, things that she hadn't known she had forgotten in the first place. She could see herself sitting in an office that she figured was within this place, talking to a man who looked rather pleased to see her. She winced as her memories started to trace back further than that moment, back to . . . the white room, where she couldn't move, where she was approached by . . . people in masks. A man . . . the same man who sat behind that desk who she was talking to . . . was there. *Welcome*, he said to her. Then, she saw herself waking up in this very room.

She knew everything now, and it made her blood boil, the anger spilling through her veins, making her body shake. *Why am I here?* she thought, *There's got to be some sort of reason.*

She came to realize that her overwhelmingly intense desire to get out almost completely shrouded her thoughts, and she could imagine nothing other than her shoving past everyone in her way and making a run for it, running as far as she could go. She pictured this over and over again until she was lifted back to reality by the sound of footsteps and the faint jingling of keys, accompanied by the sound of joyless whistling.

Day's increasingly loud, angry thoughts were interrupted by the sound of the heavy, metal door being unlocked. A man—the man from the desk—walked in, followed by two women in the uniforms that all of the staff, besides him, seemed to be wearing. He peered in at her before entering, smiling slightly, before slipping completely through the door with the two young women trailing close behind him. One of them quickened her pace to walk in front of him, setting out a small stool before him, which he proceeded to plop down onto carelessly. Day rose to her feet quickly, looking around, unsure of what to do. She stood directly across from him. The man looked up at her, smiling at her warmly with eyes that were of an unknown age. She glared at him when she noticed he was beginning to speak.

"I'm . . . Dr. Clover," he said in a familiar, sly voice, picking up on Day's discomfort and irritation.

Day only glared harder.

"We're going to begin your treatment now. Your mind won't work properly until the . . . treatment begins to work."

The room fell completely silent after he spoke those words. From a pocket in his jacket, he pulled out a plastic bag with a syringe inside of it, filled with black, swirling liquid. He flicked it a few times before reaching into another pocket, pulling out a small vial of what she assumed to be rubbing alcohol, a tourniquet, and a few cotton swabs.

Before Day could protest, he took her left hand, placing it in his lap. He rolled the sleeve up and bent her arm out, tying the tourniquet around her bicep, pulling tighter and tighter, feeling around the area, squeezing her arm until a vein showed itself. Humming softly to himself while the two women continued to stare into his back, he slowly began to empty the small vial of rubbing alcohol onto a cotton swab, which he proceeded to rub softly over her arm. The liquid felt cold, spreading chills all over her body. He flicked the top of the syringe once more before quickly feeding the needle into her arm. She gasped as pain shot through her arm, trying to look away as the black fluid filled her arm and gathered into one area.

Suddenly, it was over. Dr. Clover backed up in his chair and stood up as the two women behind him stepped up and hurried the chair out of the room. He smiled broadly, stuffing all of the used contents together into a large bag he pulled from his many pockets.

"That's it," he grinned. "We're done."

He left the room quickly after that, locking the door behind him.

Day kept waiting, and waiting, and waiting for something to happen, for some sort of symptom to show—for death. But nothing happened. She suddenly remembered what Joey had said to her, about the . . . treatment not doing anything, but she found that didn't make her feel any less uneasy. She threw herself onto the bed, and stared up at the singular fluorescent bulb until it burned her eyes and caused her to see purple splotches of nothingness everywhere she looked.

She glanced down at her arm, pressing down with her fingertips on the bruising area that the needle was inserted into. She suddenly felt a familiar strong sense of panic come over her once more, her thoughts chaotic, her vision crowded, her senses muted by the increasingly overwhelming desire to get out, to run, to be anywhere—anywhere but here inside of this room with all of these . . . weird people and treatments. She decided in that moment that she would no longer freeze up when something happened, and promised herself that the next chance she got, as soon as that huge metal door opened again, she was leaving.

But that day didn't seem to want to come. A week passed, a week that made her feel more and more as if her life were in limbo—unchanging, unmoving, with every day being the same nightmare as the day before that one. Her arm was now severely bruised and scarred, the skin on the inside of her arm beginning to scab and harden and beginning to develop a strange itch deep inside it that never seemed to go away, no matter how hard she scratched at it.

No matter how hard Day tried, she just couldn't bring herself to escape. There was never any time to do so, even if she went outside to the large, open-spaced patio with Joey. The thought of just taking off, sprinting as far away as she could away from the large white building crossed her mind multiple times, but not before the part where she actually went through with the action was shot down by her taking into account what would happen once she made it near the wall; there was no way she was getting past that. She also found there were no opportunities to explore the vast, seemingly infinite building, as everything ran on a strict schedule, and life consisted only of waking up, eating, walking around mindlessly, a "treatment" she didn't understand, and sleeping, only to do it all over again the next day. She felt herself giving up; there was no escaping this place. Joey's words had begun to make sense to her: maybe she should just embrace life here and find solace exclusively in the few glimpses of the outdoors she got, watching Samuel tenderly care for the many potted plants that lined the steps of the patio and the flower boxes scattered amongst them. Rowan, however, usually kept to herself, and sat silently on the steps while Samuel worked until he would beckon for her to move.

Day found that over time, even these small things ceased to make her happy, and the feeling of needing to leave returned with so much ferocity she could barely sleep at night. It was the only thing that ran through her head any time she saw Dr. Clover or his many assistants, which were sprinkled about in random places in the building that you would least expect to see them. In reality, they were everywhere, and Day felt alone, isolated, believing that she was the only one here who believed that everything in this place was . . . wrong. She distanced herself from them as much as possible, avoiding going to eat as much as possible so that she wouldn't have to see the sickeningly happy faces of everyone around her, seemingly oblivious to their tortuously repetitive way of life. She went days without speaking, without being present, and rather just sat and observed everything, absorbing everything about the society of people whose mentality she did not understand.

CHAPTER NINETEEN
Arrival

Leo awoke during the deep midnight hour to the sound of low voices, talking slowly, quietly—constantly. He listened through his bedroom door for a while, pressing his ear against it. The voices were coming from the parlor across from his room. The only voices he recognized were those of his parents. His stomach tied itself in knots as he heard frequent mention of his name in the hushed conversation. He could barely make any of the words out, and the words that he did hear he didn't know what they meant.

". . . We need to get this done," he heard his father's voice whisper, which intertwined with the spitting of the low flame that resided in the fireplace. "There can only be two of us, and one of them is me. There's no place for him in this."

"Please, Chester, let's wait one more year," he heard his mother say shakily.

"No. It's *him*: one of the last ones. You're lucky that he's decided to spare you, Mary."

He heard what sounded like weeping from his mother, leaving him feeling anxious and confused. Somehow, he knew this was about him, but he couldn't hear anything else they said.

Their voices grew more distant, as if they were all moving away from where they were, as if they knew he was listening in, as if they knew he was onto them.

Leo's brain was foggy. He couldn't focus on just one thing as the thoughts swimming around in his mind fell in and out of sync with one another, which were all of the questions that he knew would probably never be answered. He opened the door slightly, peeking through the small sliver of a crack. His tired vision gave everything in the adjacent brightly lit room a pulsating aura of white, causing his eyes to water. Leo's fear intensified as he realized that the two men conversing with his parents were the masked elusive figures, similar to the ones he had seen just days before. And although he hadn't seen them very many times, he felt as though he was being stalked by them constantly, day after day, in his dreams—in his own head, lurking within the dimly lit areas of his mind he dared not explore, especially not alone. He started sweating and shaking, his throat dry. He took short, panicked breaths, feeling as though he couldn't get enough air. Even though he was able to hear what they were saying clearly now, Leo couldn't concentrate on the words they were speaking, their looming shadows cast down the hallway, filling him with wonder and anxiety.

Digging his fingers into the wood, he allowed himself to open the door a bit further. This time, the door creaked loudly, causing the two anonymous men and his parents' gaze to gravitate towards his direction. Leo froze, unsure of what to do. His heart raced faster than it had ever before, and the edges of his vision began to fade to black.

Everything then seemed to happen slowly: the masked figures approached him, one on either side of his body, which was limp with terror. Their thin, cold fingers wrapped around his biceps, lifting him up and taking him away deeper into the winding corridor. Too weak to resist, he let them. Although he so badly believed, so badly he knew he could break free if he struggled and writhed enough, he let them. They had already won; he let them.

Seconds later, his eyes began to flicker shut as he was dragged gently along the floor as his parents looked on in indifference, or maybe—satisfaction. In a weak haze of exhaustion, he tried to twist himself away, and to bite and to sigh, but it seemed like these actions were only taking place inside of his head, as he realized he could no longer move his body. His eyes darted back and forth, and he couldn't control them. He couldn't scream. When his vision focused, he realized he was outside; the still neighborhood seemed to taunt him as he was hoisted over one of the men's shoulders. He blacked out completely.

CHAPTER TWENTY

It Was Seen in a Nightmare

The jolt of a car shook Leo awake. His neck hurt. Frantically, he looked around. He was in what looked to be a police car that was going uncomfortably fast along an open empty interstate. It was night. He wasn't sure what was happening, but there was one thing he knew: there was nothing he could do now. He figured he would figure out everything later and allowed the monotonous and slightly muted buzzing of the two men's voices up front lull him back to sleep.

When he awoke again, he was in a plain white room, which was cold as ice. It was empty except for a desk and two chairs facing it. He sat there in the leather-backed chair, puzzled as to why he was there. He felt alone, drowning within himself, his lungs swelling up with immense terror. He couldn't keep his legs steady; his whole body was shaking in suspense, in utter fear and shock. His sweat-covered hands gripped the arms of the chair tightly, drenching the area of fabric that he held onto. Internally, he was screaming constantly, pleading on his knees to be heard, to be let out of this strange, white world. His thoughts raced through his head, giving him a headache as his heart pounded loudly in his ears, which was the only sound that seemed to be making itself present in the small office room. Externally, he allowed his face to maintain a constant, calm disposition, tried his best to make it appear as though his shoulders were relaxed, and used every ounce of energy he had left to try to be perfectly still so that he wouldn't shake. He took slow, profound breaths, inhaling as much as he could and exhaling as slowly as possible as a last-minute attempt to calm himself down, which he knew wasn't possible, but he wanted to at least make it appear that way and to show others, who were not present within his head, that he wasn't afraid, that he wasn't nervous, that he was strong.

The same two masked men that took him from his house were positioned on either side of him, standing, looking on. Leo looked up at them, allowing wefts of anger to surface in his tone, his voice trembling as he spoke in a tone that he hoped sounded unafraid, but as soon as he started speaking, he knew he had failed at that immensely: "W-why am I here? What-what is this?"

With empty eyes, they both looked down at Leo in what appeared to be almost exact unison.

After a while, the two silent masked men left the white, dimly lit room, closing the heavy metal door behind them loudly. Leo was all alone. He looked around the small room. The desk had a built-in filing cabinet, overflowing with paperwork, most with coffee stains or severely wrinkled. There was a simple lamp near the center of the desk, the old lightbulb flickering subtly.

Suddenly, there was a loud knock on the door; Leo jumped. A tall, slender man in a dress suit popped in carrying a clipboard, greeting him with an overly broad, seemingly insincere smile that sent chills down Leo's spine. He sat down at the desk, nodding his head in acknowledgement to Leo's presence. The man began writing. When he was finished, he looked up again, crossing his legs and smiling warmly at Leo.

"Welcome," he said, his smile fading slowly. "I'm . . . Dr. Clover," he said, pulling out several bags of items from his pockets.

Leo remained silent, sweat forming on his brow. He could feel his attempts at trying to breathe calmly failing as his heart raced quicker and quicker.

The man chuckled a bit, uncrossing his legs, setting the items out onto the desk. Leo looked down at the desk and noticed a small vial of rubbing alcohol, cotton swabs, and a syringe, which was filled with clear liquid. The syringe reminded him of the one he had seen once before, in a nightmare. At least, he thought he did. Memories of that night were unclear to him, and he wanted to keep it that way. Nonetheless, Leo's eyes still widened at the sight of it, because it was familiar, and he knew that meant he had seen it somewhere. Silence hung in the air as Dr. Clover continued to situate his belongings taken from his pockets out onto the desk. After a while, he broke the silence, looking down at Leo, his eyes narrowing.

"You don't have to look so scared. I don't bite," he said finally, flashing a tooth-filled smile once more.

Leo became agitated with the man's strange attitude, no longer afraid, but rather just extremely frustrated at how he was being treated.

"Why am I here?" he blurted out without thinking.

"You need treatment. Your mind isn't working properly, not in the way I—I mean we—need it to. And until the treatment works, you must stay here so some of my assistants and I can . . . observe you, and make sure you're responding well to the treatment. Your parents have told me a lot about you, and they . . . need you here . . . It's for your own good."

This left Leo even more confused than he was before. He could feel the blood rushing to his cheeks and to the tips of his ears, leaving him feeling hot and suffocated. He thought so many things in that singular, small moment in which he felt alone, even though Dr. Clover's eyes burned into his, waiting for him to respond.

"So . . . what's going to happen to me here?" he stammered.

Dr. Clover removed his glasses and leaned in closer to him from across the desk that creaked when he moved his arms. "Well, that just depends on *you*, Leo. If your mind responds well and you do everything we ask of you, then you'll be home in no time. If you don't, then we'll have no choice but to . . . keep you here for quite a long time. Remember, we're just trying to help you."

There was a long, still silence that perpetuated in Leo's mind, even after Dr. Clover began speaking again.

"Can you hold out your arm for me, please?" the man said slyly, smiling at Leo.

In a rushed panic, Leo found himself quickly complying, jutting his left arm out quickly without even once questioning his own actions.

"Good boy."

Dr. Clover then reached for one of the air-tight bags that sat on the desk, popping it with the tip of the pen he had been writing with. He pulled out the syringe, removing the cap over the needle and tossing it to the side as he reached into another bag and pulled out the cotton swabs and the small glass bottle of rubbing alcohol. He reached into another pocket of his jacket and pulled out a tourniquet, which he tied tightly around Leo's bicep before proceeding to clean the area with the cotton swabs, which he dipped in the rubbing alcohol before applying them to Leo's chilled skin. The needle was then slowly inserted under his flesh, and the warm liquid began to course through his veins. Several moments passed.

Leo suddenly felt extremely tired. His vision blurred. His heart slowed. He no longer had the strength to hold himself up, as he felt his entire body rapidly fall numb. He allowed himself to close his eyes completely and sink to the floor.

When he awoke again, he was lying down in a bed, in a plain white room with fluorescent white light that was being emitted from a singular, small bulb in the center of the ceiling. Leo got up gently, glancing around curiously. He noticed a mirror in one corner of the room, and walked over to it slowly, his reflection staring back out at him with equal confusion. He was dressed in a red long-sleeved jumpsuit that had buttons near the top. He unbuttoned the top button so that he would feel slightly less uncomfortable in the strange attire before floating back over to the bed, sitting down at the edge, staring blankly at the pale, blank wall, imagining images in the cracks and blemishes that were covered slightly by the milky-white paint that covered the entire room. He sat there, dangling his feet off the edge of the bed for what he was certain was hours, until the bright fluorescent light's heat became too much, causing him to get up and pace around the small, cramped room.

He rolled up the sleeves of the jumpsuit, which clung to his sweaty skin. Upon rolling his sleeves up, he noticed a white bracelet wrapped tightly around the wrist of his right hand. It had a number printed on it: 3001. Leo stared at the number until it all began to blur together, the black numbers forming into a blob of nothing. He blinked hard and looked away from it just as he heard the door he hadn't noticed yet become unlocked, and then click open.

He shifted his gaze in that direction, shock paralyzing his body. A woman dressed in a rather strange uniform with many pockets lined in white stepped in. She scowled, which was the only life-like part of her face, as the rest of it seemed to remain in the same, constant dead state, which was a characteristic of most people around him that Leo had grown to be familiar with.

Without making any sort of eye contact with him, she walked deeper into the room, deeper and deeper until she was standing directly in front of him. The woman pointed towards the opened door, gesturing for him to step out of the room. Leo was pulled toward her waving hand, as he had begun to follow her almost immediately. She led him down a long white, winding corridor, until they reached a wide-open room in which seemingly countless people sat around round tables. The noise in the room was such a large contrast to the area of the building from which he had just come from that Leo winced at the noise and was tempted to cover his ears, to shield himself from the sound of what sounded like thousands of chattering voices.

He glanced around at all the tables filled with people, overwhelmed. He looked desperately around for a place to sit, as he found that he was the only one standing up. He felt his cheeks turn red as many people, who were also dressed in the same attire as him, looked up periodically, their eyes darting away from his direction any time he took notice of them staring. They exchanged amused glances with each other, entertained by the newcomer's confusion.

He walked over to a random table, keeping his head down as he weaved through the maze of round tables until he got to the one that he chose, hesitant to look up, as he knew the people who were sitting there would look at him the same as most of the room had when he had first walked in. Leo was afraid, afraid to make any contact whatsoever with these . . . strangers, and the feeling of fear only intensified as he waited longer and longer to look up. Eventually, he decided he was going to have to eventually—otherwise he might come off as weird, and somehow that made him slightly more uneasy than the general idea of being kept here did.

Slowly, Leo raised his head, glancing around at the people sitting around him at the table. To his delight, no one was looking at him, and no one was even facing in his direction, as they had all begun to talk amongst each other quietly. He was beginning to think that they didn't even know if he was there at all. Now that he had gotten what he had wanted, he wasn't sure if this *was* what he wanted. He couldn't decide which made him feel more uncomfortable: not being noticed, or talking to people he didn't know. He decided that there would be an awkward conversation in store for him once everyone decided to look in his direction and then notice him. So, he realized he'd rather make himself acknowledged now, rather than waiting for it to become weird. To no one in particular, he began speaking, hoping that someone would hear him.

"Hey. I'm Leo . . ."

Leo's voice trailed off, the dense air of the white room holding in the quiet of his voice, squeezing it tight.

No one responded. Leo's heart sank, recognizing his voice had blended in all too well with the constant audible tangle of words that filled the lively air of the room. To his surprise, the boy sitting next to him whipped around and smiled at him, sporting a wide, friendly grin. Leo immediately took notice of his alarmingly bright red hair.

"Hi. I'm Joey," he said in a loud chipper voice.

Leo thought he looked nothing like the sound of his voice.

There was silence.

"So . . . you just got here, didn't you?"

Leo nodded.

"Yeah, that's what I thought," he laughed.

Joey tapped the boy sitting next to him lightly on the shoulder, getting his attention, and began talking to him in a slightly hushed tone.

"This is the third one this week, Aiden. That's kinda weird, don'tcha think? We don't usually get this many new people at once."

Aiden shrugged, his shoulder-length platinum blonde, almost white hair rising and falling with his shoulders.

He stared at Leo, furrowing his brow. He whispered something inaudible to Joey, before casting his gaze back onto Leo. Joey cleared his throat and smiled. "Leo, this is my twin, Aiden. Say hi, Aiden."

Aiden scowled, rolling his eyes before looking away. Joey grabbed Aiden's arm and made a waving motion with it. Aiden gave him a sidelong glance but didn't seem to mind all that much.

Leo forced a smile before looking away, confused. . . . *Third one this week?* he thought. It didn't make any sense to him, and everything he saw and heard around him sent him further and further into an intense panic, which he knew would become too much for him to handle eventually. His mind drifted back to how he felt when he kept hallucinating—no, *seeing*—that woman in his room. The thought of those sleepless, torturous nights was becoming increasingly vivid, and his mind had begun to apply those feelings to what was happening to him now, and worst of all, there was nothing he could do about it—nothing. He tried his hardest to continue to talk to Joey, trying his best to ignore Aiden's brooding stares. He lowered his voice.

"Look, I need to get out of here, I don't know why I'm—"

Joey cut him off, laughing. He put his arm around him. "You can't get out until you receive treatment. Like, lots of it. Sometimes *years of it*. It doesn't always work right away. You gotta wait. Aiden and I are still waiting for it to do . . . whatever it's supposed to do. We've been here eleven years . . ."

Leo's head was spinning, and he could barely even hear any more of Joey's words. Everything suddenly seemed so loud within his head, within his body. He got up, walking to another section of the room, leaving his new 'friend' with Aiden, the quiet sound of their mumbling almost completely lost in all of the noise. He began following a group of people through a set of doors on the other side of the room, which opened up into another hallway, a lobby area, and then through another set of doors that led to a patio area, with a clear view of a wide open space of freshly cut grass and foliage, which was stopped abruptly by a cement wall that closed it all in. Way more people were outside than he had expected, which filled him with suffocating anxiety that he was being watched, that his every move was being monitored closely, being judged intensely. There were what seemed like endless clusters of people in red, moving about constantly in their seemingly designated groups—talking, laughing.

Suddenly, he noticed someone, far away, standing alone, no one remotely close to him. Slowly, he walked over to him, careful to not make it obvious. He stopped when he thought if he were to take another step it would be too close. He squinted as hard as he could. Was that . . . it couldn't be. He looked exactly like . . . Willie.

Leo wanted to have a closer look, because the resemblance was uncanny. Just as he took another step in his direction, a loud noise sounded from back inside of the building. The familiar face was lost in the crowd of people forming around the double doors near the steps, pushing to get back inside. Leo looked around for him one last time before giving up completely and following everyone back inside. They all walked back to the room with the round tables, but this time, instead of sitting down, they began forming a group near and around a large cart that held many plates of food on it.

Upon catching a glance of what everyone was so excited about, Leo walked back to the seat at the table he had claimed as his when he first entered the room and sat back down. He wasn't hungry. Just the thought of eating in this place made him sick. He watched as everyone that had been sitting at that same table he was sitting at returned, and along with them was Joey, who reached down and ruffled his hair with one hand, holding a plate of food with the other. "Hey, why'd you run away from me, Leo?" he asked him jokingly.

Leo didn't answer; he was far too deep inside of his head now, too deep inside to hear anything that was being said. He just wanted to get out. He felt as though he had a lot to think about, and no thinking could be done when he was near others, and especially not when others were actually talking to him. The only person he had interest in talking to now was himself, and he couldn't even do that. He put his head down on the table, glancing around the white room sprinkled with red people hurrying about. He drummed his fingers against the table lightly for what felt like an eternity, waiting for something—anything—to happen.

After a long while, the same loud noise from earlier sounded loudly above their heads, making Leo jump and quickly sit up to try to find the source of the loud ringing. Suddenly, everyone got up from the tables, leaving their empty plates in their places, and began filing out the double doors that led to the confusingly narrow hallway. Puzzled, Leo figured he should just go along with the group, making sure that he wasn't drawing any attention to himself by looking ignorant. Another set of doors was opened, revealing the hallway of small rooms he felt he had just come from. Before entering their rooms, some people said their goodbyes to each other, while others lifelessly entered without saying a word, their bleary eyes staring straight ahead. He glanced at the numbers on the doors, which were all in the five thousands. He assumed the bracelet he had been given was his room number, so he walked through the winding hallways, exploring every extra corridor, every subsection until, out of sheer luck, he managed to find room 3001. He opened the unlocked heavy door slowly, pushing it as hard as he could. It locked behind him loudly.

Even before Leo could panic, or even sit down, he heard the door unlock, and in walked a man he did not recognize, followed by two women in matching attire. The man smirked at him. One of the women stepped forward, placing a stool in front of the man, which he proceeded to sit down on, directly in front of Leo. The room was quiet. Suddenly, the man who he did not recognize spoke in a low, steady voice.

"Hello. It's time for your treatment."

Leo tried his best to maintain a calm exterior disposition.

"Do you remember who I am?" the man asked him, smiling slyly. "I'm Dr. Clover."

Leo blinked. He did not know this man. Should he know him?

". . . No," he answered slowly.

Dr. Clover smiled.

Suddenly, Leo felt an intense pain that began deep inside of his head, shooting pain outwards, down all over his body. Many memories from what seemed like long ago began to come back to him, cluttering his already chaotic mind. He remembered this man now. He found it strange how just moments ago, he had no memory of him at all.

"W-wait, yes—yes I do," he stammered, correcting himself quickly.

The man's smile drifted slowly down his face, turning into a deep, sour, unsettling scowl.

Leo could feel the beads of sweat gathering on his forehead as his heart pounded in his ears, and he clenched his fists so tightly he was certain his fingernails would tear holes in his flesh.

Dr. Clover turned around to look at one of the women, who raised the clipboard she was carrying to her chest, clicking the pen open and making a singular mark on a paper that Leo could not see. Dr. Clover clenched his jaw tight and squinted his eyes slightly, appearing annoyed and concerned at the same time. He sighed deeply before he began speaking again.

"I'm going to give you your treatment now."

Leo breathed deeply and remained silent as Dr. Clover pulled out the same items from his coat pockets as he had done before. This time, one thing was different. Instead of the syringe being filled with clear, seemingly harmless liquid, it was now filled with thick, black fluid that Leo knew he had seen once before—in a dream—no, in a nightmare. He held his breath as Dr. Clover began the same procedure as he did when Leo was in the office. He watched as the fluid gathered under his skin near the injection area, causing his top layer of skin to swell and appear darker. He looked away when the man pressed down on the sensitive area to make the fluid within his arm disperse within him. He closed his eyes tightly. Suddenly, it was over. He heard Dr. Clover stand up and pick up the chair he had been sitting in, making his way out the door, locking it behind him. Leo stared at his arm in confusion, watching as the swollen area became smaller and smaller. His head spun as images of death flashed through his mind, of Day. The silence that hung heavy in the room turned into a screaming wail that droned on, growing louder and louder, until—there was nothing.

CHAPTER TWENTY-ONE
January 5, 1980

Five years had passed since Leo's arrival—five long, tedious years of waiting, anxiously suffering, and more waiting, for something he did not know of, but something he had been waiting for, for years, constantly finding himself yearning for something—*anything*—to happen. He knew that today would be different, although he didn't actually know for sure, as he thought that same thing about every day he spent here, delighting in even the most miniscule of events.

Per usual, when Leo heard the sound of the heavy door that contained him within the small white room click open, he stumbled sleepily through the metal door, making his way through the halls and into the room with all of the round tables, the room with all of the people, the room in which he talked with Joey, and many other people he wasn't very fond of. Over the years, some of them had gone, never to be seen again. He wondered what became of them. Mostly, however, the crowd was the same. Today when he sat down, he realized that everyone around him was here much earlier than usual, as he usually arrived much sooner than everyone else, eager to get the day over with, and get back to waiting for his time to end, whether it was through somehow making it over the giant wall and over the hedge, or through death; he was certain he would be more than satisfied with either of the two happening, oftentimes preferring the latter.

He looked around at everyone's melancholic faces, which were all usually so joyful and non-contemplative. Today, they looked as though they had learned where they were, they looked as though they were finally living in the world Leo lived in: reality. He looked over at Joey, who looked the most mournful of all.

"What's wrong?"

"Rowan. She's dead."

Leo remembered her: the frail, old woman that sat at the table with them, along with a few others that he never had an interest in talking to. He said nothing, allowing Joey to continue talking after a long pause. There seemed to be a barrier, an atmosphere around their table completely different to that of others. It was otherworldly how different it was; stagnating, sad air was present, while about them there was life, and noise and laughter.

"There's a rumor that . . . the treatment can kill; that it can weaken you to the point where . . . you die, especially after so many years of taking it."

Joey's words sent a potent chill down Leo's spine, causing his head to spin as it filled with questions he would never have the answers to, making him feel faint, shaky, nauseous.

Suddenly, Joey leaned in, scooting his chair out so that he would be closer to Leo and in a hushed, wavering voice, he spoke to him slowly.

"I'm gonna be real with you," he said, his easygoing nature distorting into a neurotic blob of words, "I'm scared. Like, you've been here for a while now and . . . me and Aiden have been here *way* longer than you have. What if we're—what if all of us—are gonna die?"

Leo looked into Joey's deep brown pools for eyes, desperately trying to understand why he, of all people, was suddenly so distressed. Leo found that he didn't much care what happened to him, as he began to think about which he would favor more: escape forever or spending the rest of his life . . . *here* . . . and die. He looked away from Joey's eyes quickly, suddenly beginning to listen to himself, biting his lip hard in stress, shaking his head.

No, he thought, *there's an escape from this place, and if there isn't . . . I'll make one. I don't care how long it takes; I can't stay here anymore. I just can't.*

He narrowed his eyes at Joey, thinking. To Joey, however, this came across as skepticism. In imagined defeat, he shrank back, dropping his shoulders.

Joey sighed.

"Well . . . why else would she be dead?"

Leo shrugged, mimicking his sigh. He couldn't focus. "Yeah, see?"

After what felt like no time at all, the familiar noise sounded from an unknown location, signaling everyone to go back to their designated rooms. Leo walked in silence next to Aiden and Joey until they all split up to go to their different areas.

When he entered his room, he sat on the edge of the bed, waiting until Dr. Clover entered, providing him with another syringe filled with a substance that he did not know the name of, adding another scar in the crease of his arm that would sit among the countless others—a starry night sky of pinpricks, each a memento of each day he spent here. He prepared himself, sitting up straighter, hands in his lap, prepared to endure yet another futile attempt at treatment.

He looked on as Dr. Clover walked in right on time, just as he had expected him to.

But something was off—extremely off. The smile that always greeted Leo that Dr. Clover wore on his face wasn't there, and in its place was a tense, emotionless knot of an expression, scowling at Leo from behind a pair of thin-framed glasses. The two assistants that he always seemed to have with him weren't there, and he was carrying the chair he always sat in himself. He sat in front of Leo as usual, but this time cast his gaze downward. He parted his lips.

"We're going to be . . . doing something a little different today," he said in a rushed voice, crossing one slender leg tightly over the other.

"Since our treatment hasn't been working on you, we're just going to do a little blood test to . . . test for something."

He scowled, narrowing his lips in apparent frustration.

Leo didn't say a word, allowing the white room to flood with a passionate, red anger, the same color he knew Dr. Clover was thinking.

From his pockets, he pulled out several empty blood collection tubes, the all-too-familiar syringe, and needles of various sizes. While he began the process of everything, Leo turned his head towards the ceiling, his head spinning with worry—fear, an intense fear that had been brought on by the look on Dr. Clover's face, as it was one he did not recognize, nor was it one he wanted to recognize. The thought of the enigmatic man already made him uneasy, but his deep, hardened scowl was what really, *really* did it. It was times like these within this place when his mind began to wander, wandering far off into the past, revisiting places he did not want to go—ever. It took him back to Day, back to his attic, back to her dead body, back to those journal entries, back to . . . the warehouse. Sometimes, it was a combination of all of these things that proceeded to attack him all at once, engulfing him in a sea of . . . fury. It was no longer sadness numbed down by distractions, diluted by other feelings, but rather pure anger, fueled by fear, by confusion.

As Dr. Clover began to draw his blood, Leo averted his gaze, staring deeply into the wall on the left side of him. This did little to calm his nerves and did even less to distract him from the uncomfortable, pinching sensation in his arm as his rage-filled blood was reaped from his veins.

He found that he was beginning to feel faint just as Dr. Clover finished filling the last small vial, removing the tourniquet, and slowly removing the thick needle from the inside of his arm. He gathered the vials up, placing them in a bag, which he proceeded to place inside one of his jacket pockets, along with everything else.

"I'll be right back," he said coldly as he began to leave the room, dragging the chair along, locking the door behind him when he finally made it out.

Leo broke out into a cold sweat, swallowing hard, his dry throat making his mouth feel small and cramped. His shoulders tingled as they began to tense up, his whole body shaking with anxiety, with fear. He told himself over and over that he had nothing to worry about, and that nothing was wrong, but nothing he said seemed to be able to calm his heart, which threatened over and over to burst out of his ribcage, a feeling that would only be slightly worse than how his irrational thoughts were making him feel, which was paralyzed, motionless—lifeless. He lay down flat on his back in a desperate attempt to soothe his churning stomach, which fluttered with every new thought that surfaced itself into his consciousness. He allowed his eyes to close slowly, suddenly feeling weak and heavy.

Why am I here? he thought to himself over and over, only giving him greater, more pronounced feelings of uneasiness.

Just as his eyes flickered open, he heard Dr. Clover returning. He could hear him on the other side of the metal door, desperately fumbling to get the lock open before finally bursting inside, his face twisted into an indescribably furious expression, harboring an unfathomable amount of rage. His mouth was distorted into a snarling, yet open-mouthed scowl, his eyes small, his eyebrows sitting low on his face and pushed extremely close together tensely.

Leo sat up quickly, backing up against the wall in terror as Dr. Clover walked up to him hurriedly, clearly in a blind rage. Noticing Leo's extreme panic, he forced himself to calm down slightly, controlling his breathing.

"I have some . . . bad news," he said through his teeth. "I'm afraid that . . . since the treatment isn't working, you can no longer be kept here. And . . . since I don't allow any risks of any . . . whistleblowers going out and telling everyone what I am doing here . . . today is . . . your last day."

Leo suddenly couldn't breathe. His throat tightened, as he began breathing faster and faster. His lungs felt as though they were going to burst when he tried to take deeper breaths. His whole body shook as a feeling of dread washed over him, causing him to tense up. He clenched his fists tightly, the sweat that encased his palms causing them to constantly slip. *No. No. No. No. No. No. No. This can't be happening.*

"W-why?" he blurted out without thinking.

"Because you're . . . resilient. Just like an Acheron!" Dr. Clover snarled back, seeming to instantly regret his words.

He slowly felt himself losing consciousness, his body growing weaker, until suddenly many thoughts began piling into his vacant head. He began . . . remembering things, many things that he thought he had forgotten. He thought back to when he read the journal, the name on the cover, the sprawled letters physical representations of the writer's madness. He remembered . . . Acheron . . . Alois Acheron. It didn't make sense. The name on the cover . . . Floyd . . .

He began slowly piecing everything together in his mind, sweat gathering on his brow as Dr. Clover's eyes—daggers—cut into his.

"You're—you're Floyd?" he stammered, his bottom lip quivering.

"What did you say?" Floyd snapped, baring teeth as he yelled at him.

"Th-the journal! I know—I think I know who you are! Wh-what are you doing?"

Before Leo could finish speaking, Floyd left the room in a hurried panic, dropping a few unused syringes in bags from his pockets as he floated away.

CHAPTER TWENTY-TWO
Switchblade

Leo paced around the small, white room, his bare feet treading heavily over the cold marble floor. He suddenly felt even more hopeless, helpless; had he missed his chance? Or was his time to act taken from him long ago when he had so many conflicting thoughts that he couldn't decide what to do? Whichever of the two fate had handpicked for him, he winced in defeat, hugging his frail body toward him as he shivered with anxiety. The feeling of damnation by Clover—or Floyd's words spun through his head as he tried to make sense of what he thought was happening, and what would happen, which left him feeling even more trapped than he already was, because this time, he couldn't think of anything to ease his throbbing head, which pulsated constantly with the thought that, in a matter of hours, he was going to die. That thought alone was enough to make him want to throw himself against one of the cement walls over and over again, to just get it over with. He couldn't live with the anticipation—he just couldn't. Dying was all he could think about anymore. It was easy to make himself hyper-fixate on one singular thing, since there was absolutely nothing else to do in the small, square room. Within the room, his mind took over him, controlling him, not allowing him to escape, no matter how badly he wanted it.

Suddenly, Leo began coughing. He couldn't stop. His lungs felt as though they were filling with phlegm, with fluid, making it harder and harder to breathe. *Is this it?* He kept coughing and coughing until he tasted blood on his tongue. His eyes began to water. He looked around and noticed that the room was slowly filling with smoke. The source of it seemed to be through a pipe that was fed through a small hole in the wall furthest away from him. Leo's muscles felt weak, and he fluttered slowly to the ground. He could no longer move, not even slightly, and he found that he barely even had the strength to blink. Although he was familiar with this enigmatic sensation, his eyes closed slowly, and he allowed himself to let go, too exhausted to think about his fear that this was the end.

When he awoke again, he was strapped tightly to a chair in a wide-open space, fluorescent lights hanging above his head. All at once, all of the lights turned off—all except for one, which was the one directly over his head. The light pulsated with his fluttering heart. He looked up at it, sweating profusely in the heat. When he heard what sounded like many footsteps approaching him quickly, he began desperately trying to break free of the restraints, unsuccessful, leaving only red marks of effort etched into his wrists. He looked on in immense terror as a group of people in various types of masks, clad in robes, approached him quickly, emerging from the dark areas of the room. There were at least twenty of them, the overwhelmingly loud noise of their seemingly light-hearted, yet monotonous chatter filling Leo with unfathomable amounts of nervousness and fear of what would happen next.

The crowd then began parting, and Dr. Clover—Floyd—walked slowly down the open space created by the masked individuals. He was holding a syringe that was much larger than the ones he had used in the past. Everyone around him walked with him, nearing closer and closer until they were all directly in front of his face. Leo closed his eyes, waiting for death, silently wishing for it to just hurry up and take him. He heard Floyd remove the cap and flick the top of the syringe quickly in one effortlessly fluid motion. He felt the needle meet his flesh, and squinted his eyes shut tightly. This was it.

"Stop!" an unrecognizable voice that belonged to a woman yelled, shattering the silence, causing a flare of noise to arise from everyone in the room.

Floyd lifted the needle from Leo's flesh, whipping around to see who the protesting shout belonged to. Floyd flared his nostrils and tightened his lips, breathing hard.

Every one of the people in masks turned their heads to face a person in a plain white mask, making it a point to turn their whole bodies in that direction too, as to not be falsely blamed for speaking out against something that had to be done. Being blamed would mean facing Floyd's full wrath. They seemed to cower as the doctor with the syringe delivered menacing looks through the masked menagerie, parting them even further.

The woman stepped forward and removed the white mask. When Leo saw her face, he suddenly felt . . . different. He knew who she was, although she looked different now, but also the same—it was his mother. She hadn't appeared to have aged in the slightest. The light seemed to form a halo around her messy dark brown hair as the desperation in her voice grew more apparent. Leo's eyes widened.

"Floyd, please, you can't do this!" she cried. She pulled out a tiny switchblade from within one of the folds of the long robe she wore, and ran over to him quickly, digging the knife into the leather straps that held him down to the chair.

"Go! Leave!" she yelled, as she was beginning to be restrained by the surrounding people in masks.

Floyd stood back as everything descended into chaos, and everyone surrounded her, trying to stop her from running away. Too stunned to move, Leo sat in the chair, looking on in horror as things began to turn violent. Another person in a plain red mask that resembled a cat tore their mask off.

"Mary, what are you doing!" his voice boomed, knocking the small knife out of her hands. It fell to the floor loudly, before the noise ceased to exist, blending in with the sound of discord that filled the huge room. As he continued to yell at her, Leo quickly realized that the man was his father. Time had also left him completely unaffected. Next to him stood Mr. Everett, unmasked, his expression hollow.

. . . *Willie . . . where is he?*

Suddenly, Floyd snapped his fingers, and everything went silent, and everyone became completely still. In an unnaturally calm voice, he began to speak to Mary slowly, clearly trying his hardest to hide his anger.

"You lied to me," he said through gritted teeth, "You said you would bring him to me, to let me treat him. I've given you so many chances. I've been watching him. I know his potential as one of them. He would make me so powerful. But now that you've waited so long, his potential is significantly weakened. Do you know how much time you've wasted? You were chosen to be spared, and *this* is how you repay the Rosarium?" He was shouting now as he continued while Mary stood frozen, seemingly hypnotized by his voice that tore through the room like a bullet, that oscillated throughout the entire building, ricocheting from the stout ceiling.

Regaining her ability to move, Mary backed away in a panic, making her way toward a door that led out of the room, a door that wasn't visible to Leo from where he was sitting; the darkness shielded it from him. Floyd slowly walked towards her, and raised his arm up, high over his head. Mary gargled out a scream as she was suddenly lifted high off the ground and thrown against the cement brick wall with an unimaginable force. Her eyes became lifeless and dull, staring out into nothing as she fell slowly to the floor, her body twisted contrapposto, in an almost pleading stance. In that moment—in that one moment—she was the very picture of elegance.

Everyone looked at her, unable to avert their eyes, unable to move. Floyd watched her body for several long moments, as if he expected her to rise again, smirking as though he wanted it to happen just so he could experience the pleasure of watching the life fade from her bleak face once more.

Too paralyzed to move, Leo stared into Floyd's darting eyes as he spoke.

"Leo," he began. "I insured you would experience a . . . gradual curiosity, an unquenchable itch that would eventually lead you right to me. And it worked," he beamed, as he continued his speech, booming through the silence. "Did you like all of the hints I left for you? In your attic, in the warehouse. And what became of your . . . friend." he trailed off. Leo could only assume that he meant Day. Floyd continued, gesturing to Mr. Everett, "he did an excellent job executing that for us. I couldn't help but mess with you. I wanted to have you. All three of you. Your friends? You all have this . . . ability, an ability that begs to be tampered with, and harnessed. But her death? It was fake, a farce. They're both here. They have been for years. Right with you. I kept you separate. I bet you thought they were dead. Did you believe it? Did you believe it, Leo?"

With a burst of adrenaline and rage, Leo sprang up from the chair, making a run for the door his mother had tried to open before meeting her fruitless demise. He was just a few feet away from it when Chester grabbed him by the shoulders, wrapping his arms tightly around his neck, desperately trying to drag him back to the chair. He looked over to Floyd, as if seeking approval. Floyd nodded, gesturing to the chair that painfully detained him.

"Good, son, now put him back. We can't have anyone leaving so soon, can we?" he said slyly, turning to face Leo.

Leo was stunned; why did his parents have . . . emotion? He thought back to how lifelessly still and unresponsive they were, shuddering. As he was dragged closer and closer back to the chair, he began to devise a plan to get out of the door that lingered so close, yet so far away from him. Seeming to take notice of Leo's darting eyes, Floyd began talking to him from the center of the room.

"Yes, I'm Floyd. But I guess you know that?" he chuckled through his teeth. "I must create my . . . perfect world, and long ago, I chose Thornbrook." He paced around, his loyals carefully orienting their bodies towards him with every step he took. "And those that are immune to my power, those that . . . *truly think* . . . for themselves . . . can simply not be here any longer. I want my world to be perfect. I have found it gives me power the more I collect. It gives me life eternal." He walked towards a huddled group of the masked, stroking their chins. "They keep me alive, simply by existing. They do not think; *I* think for them, all of my roses—and they like it." Floyd grinned, almost giddy talking about his creations, standing on his tiptoes briefly, before lowering his lanky body back down to earth.

Chester sat Leo back in the chair, desperately trying to figure out how he was meant to detain him in it. Floyd briskly walked over to them, his coat creating a slight chill in the air behind him. He placed his large hand on Leo's head and squeezed. "You, however, are special; you have a mind that has the ability to create this . . . noise, this resounding din. You think loudly, and if I could have you . . . I would become unfathomably powerful; unstoppably powerful. However," He squeezed tighter. "*Mary*—your mother—she ruined it all. She stalled me, and waited, and stalled some more because you are her only son. She loves you. She doesn't want you to become a rose, even though she took a pact in order to spare herself, under the condition that she marry my son and continue the Rosarium should I no longer be able to. But because she waited, your . . . unique ability is faded. You're no longer of use to me, Leo. We can't have that," he whispered, grimacing. "Now, for my final . . . treatment. Are you ready?" he hissed slyly as he attempted to repair the slashed leather cuffs on the chair.

With that, Leo sprung up, dashing past both Chester and Floyd's unsuspecting faces, flailing his arms as he felt their hands grabbing at him. Suddenly, Floyd grabbed hold of him, his hands around his neck, pulling tighter as he attempted to drag him back. However, somehow, Leo was stronger; he managed to untangle himself from Floyd's grasp, pushing his body off of his, throwing him into the ground hard.

While Floyd struggled to regain the strength to stand up, he ran back to the area near the chair, grabbing the switchblade that fell to the ground during his and Mary's struggle. Without a sound, Floyd lunged himself at Leo, startling him, causing his off-guard body to fall to the ground, with Floyd on top of him. The onlookers backed away as far as they could, pressing themselves up against the wall farthest away from the two. Floyd shoved Leo's face into the ground, desperately trying to get him to stay down, digging his thumbs deep into the sides of his neck until his face turned purple and his eyes began to water.

In a final attempt to save his life, Leo drove the switchblade deeply into Floyd's back, watching as the life faded from his eyes. He threw his body to the side and sat up, covered in sweat, breathing hard.

Suddenly, Floyd's body began to shake violently, and Leo watched as his middle-aged facial features began to age rapidly, his cheekbones sinking in, new wrinkles forming in places in which there were none. He became older and older, his skin becoming more and more loose, until it began falling off of his bones, the remains falling to the ground in a large pile of ash.

Everyone glanced around as though they had suddenly realized where they were. Their eyes, which peered through the holes in their masks, were no longer glazed over and lifeless, no staring off into nothing, as if there was something alive trapped behind them. The people were alive, and began mumbling things amongst each other before walking hurriedly out of the room, with his father leading the way, walking quicker than the rest, eager to escape his mistakes.

Leo shakily climbed to his feet and began weeping, the tears burning into the wounds on his face, causing him to wince. He looked down at his shaking hands, at the tiny switchblade, both of which were covered in blood—Floyd's blood. He couldn't believe what he had done.

He sank to his knees, curling himself up, throwing the knife across the floor. The longer he stayed there, the more his guilt shrunk, and the more he realized he felt nothing. There was nothing.

CHAPTER TWENTY-THREE
Switch

Willie massaged his temples slowly, tiredly stepping out of the pale white room and into the hallway, navigating quickly through the winding narrow passages, eager to reach the lobby and then leave through the double-doors to get outside, only to stare out onto the lawn and out past the wall that towered high above him, while he would sit down on the crumbling pavement and watch the wind blow through the many plants that sat alongside him, joining his solitude. When he reached the outside, he sat down, his back against the side of the building, watching the people he had been here with for years but never talked to standing together, whispering things he would never know, talking to other people he would never know.

Aiden stood near the door also, startling him as he began to speak with people he had never seen before. He glared angrily over at them as the sound of their voices began drowning out everything else entirely. He wasn't particularly fond of Aiden, as his silently brooding, rude disposition was seemingly the only element to his personality. Willie wasn't one for talking either; he hadn't talked to anyone throughout his entire stay here, but at least he didn't shoot menacing, hateful glances towards unsuspecting people who weren't even paying him any attention in the slightest before being provoked by a single stare that held so much power.

He crossed his arms, looked in the opposite direction, and began listening in on the group's boisterous conversation, picking up minimal amounts of sentences that were mostly just singular words or brief phrases. The conversation seemed redundant at first, before it drifted onto the topic of what had happened to Rowan a couple of days ago, which Willie had only heard a few things about; he didn't much care for her anyway, as they had barely spoken once.

"Yeah, they just took her and . . ."

"She's dead," another unfamiliar voice finished for the other.

"Well, at least now she's better off than she was," Aiden said slowly, "and at least she was way less of a neurotic mess than . . . Day."

At the sound of her name, Willie turned his head slowly to face them, his interest peaking. Although he couldn't remember the last time he had organically thought about Day, he often liked to think she was here too. He would go so far as to say he had caught fleeting glances of her through dense crowds, and even Leo. Ghosts.

"Who?" someone asked, their voice trailing off when Aiden looked over at him with a patronizing stare.

". . . Never mind," Aiden mumbled before walking away to sit on one of the wide steps that led toward the open field of grass. The group of people that he was talking to started to look around, as though they were lost, before dispersing entirely, going off in every direction. Some remained outside, and some walked back into the building.

Without thinking, Willie ran and sat next to Aiden on the steps, many thoughts drifting through his head, screaming for an explanation, desperate to hear more about Day, whom he knew was gone, gone forever. It was painfully unclear to him why Aiden—someone who never knew her at all—would know anything at all about her, let alone her name or something she did. He breathed deeply and began speaking.

"So . . . you said you knew Day?"

Aiden looked up, scowling at him.

"What are you talking about? *Knew?* She's here."

Willie's eyes went wide, his lips parting to speak, but then closing again. He couldn't find any words.

"W-what?" he stammered, his voice shaky.

Aiden wrinkled his face in confusion.

". . . Yeah. She just . . . doesn't come out of her room anymore. Wait. Here she is now."

The two looked up in unison as Day slowly stepped through the door, looking around nervously. Willie watched her float through the grass, her frail legs carrying her gently through the tall blades absorbing her. He could barely recognize her, but he knew it was her by her cascading black curls and dainty round face that didn't seem to have changed at all. Without thinking, he ran over to her as quickly as he could.

"Day. It's me," he said quietly as tears began clouding his vision.

Her eyes widened, and she smiled broadly, instantly recognizing Willie's unforgettable way of speaking, He pulled her into a long embrace as she rubbed his back with her hands, feeling his long hair that he had draped behind his back. After what felt like an eternity, Willie pulled away, staring into her eyes deeply, unblinking. He took her hands in his, squeezing them gently as he studied her face, her delicate lips tempting him.

"I . . . I thought you were dead," he said softly, continuing to hold tightly onto her hands.

"Me too."

There was a loud thundering of many bare feet pounding against the pavement, rushing to get outside. Willie and Day watched in awe as everything became happily chaotic, people of all ages running about like children, using each other to jump over the wall, while others could be seen leaving on the other side of the building once they had managed to get the door open to leave through the small office. When the crowd cleared, Leo stood alone , instantly meeting Willie's gaze. He knew this person, and he knew for a fact it was Willie, his long hair and slender body a trademark. He walked over to them, a smile slowly spreading across his face.

"I did it," he breathed, tears filling his eyes as he took them both into his arms, holding onto them tightly.

"Did what?" Willie asked quickly.

"Freed us. Freed everyone. He's dead."

They both knew who he was talking about, and, too eager to leave, they decided not to question anything about how, or what happened, as everything in that moment was very fragile. Sealed together through a burst of chaos, the three walked silently side by side, tucking away their thoughts, their experiences. An unspoken bond told them that, together, they already knew everything that had happened to one another, their fates similar, if not exactly the same. They walked slowly to the office, opening the door adjacent to the door, which led to an area outside of the wall. Here, they found everyone else that had left sprinkled across the edges of the seemingly abandoned highway, walking quickly with no sense of direction, but with a single purpose in mind, which was to get as far away as they could from the building that locked them away from the world for so long.

The three drifted over to a sidewalk that was partially shrouded in shade and walked until they reached a familiar area. Leo led them back to the area that he remembered to be their neighborhood, surprised at how close by it was. They hiked through the now overgrown area behind the cul-de-sac, the river now barely visible through all of the brush and undergrowth that covered it. Willie reached for Day's hand, grasping it hesitantly as a cold wind rushed through the trees, tousling their hair, summoning goosebumps. The only sound that could be heard was the sound of twigs breaking beneath their bare feet, and the crunching of dying leaves. Leo quickened his pace when his feet began to tingle in the cold, falling numb as they continued to walk through the dense woodland area, a light snow beginning to fall from the gray sky. When he finally saw his house, he started running, with Willie and Day following close behind. He walked up the steps slowly, reaching under the mat and grabbing the key, chilled by the wintery air. He felt something else underneath the mat. Shivering, he lifted it up completely, revealing a single piece of paper with rushed words scrawled onto it. With numb, shaking hands, he read it slowly to himself while Day and Willie looked on over his shoulder.

> Leo,
> I'm sorry. I'm sorry, I'm sorry. You won't be hearing from me any longer. Take this place. It's yours now. You were special. I tried my hardest to keep you away from your friends, but it seems they have found you. Sunlight always draws the weeds near.
> —Chester Kaylock

Leo read it over and over, seething with anger. He ripped it up into the tiniest pieces possible and threw them into the air, watching them blend in with the snowflakes that plummeted to the ground around them.

They looked at him, confusion filling their freezing faces. Leo just shook his head over and over and proceeded to open the door.

There was silence, and only silence, all except for the crackling fire that the three sat around. No one could manage to utter even a singular word. The wind whistling aggressively through the trees could be heard from inside of the house, vibrating the old windows as a raging storm was beginning to develop outside. There was nothing left for him here—nothing.

Days later, while he was sauntering around in a haze, trying to understand all of his thoughts, everything he had heard, and his world, he walked over to the river—what was left of it—and found Willie. He smiled as he found himself beginning to remember all the times, which felt like centuries ago, when he would sit in that very spot and talk with him for hours. He felt so distant to him now, the frigid air matching the distance between their hearts. He lost him. He had lost both of them, and he knew it. Nonetheless, he slid down next to him, staring down into the geometric patterns made by the murky water, which had frozen over.

". . . What are you gonna do?" Willie asked him innocently.

Leo's thoughts swarmed, consuming him. There were too many. He couldn't think of anything. Despite being free, he still had an overwhelming desire to get out. He didn't understand it, nor did he know how he would get out of a place that he wasn't contained in, a place that didn't even exist. So many unanswered questions, accompanied by unwanted answers. He couldn't hear anything. He swallowed hard, standing up abruptly. He swallowed the lump in his throat and tried his best to speak in a steady voice, not allowing anything to escape from within, speaking as he walked away.

"I'm fine. I'll do just fine. I'll get out someday."

He walked and began running and running until he felt his lungs would burst.

Days, months, years passed since he had begun running. And he would continue to run, run away from things that were nonexistent, yet lacking the ability to cease to exist. And they never, ever would.

ABOUT THE AUTHOR

ABOUT THE AUTHOR

Ambrea Richardson is a native to Atlanta, Georgia. She has a passion for horror and the macabre, and enjoys writing short stories in her free time. When she isn't writing, she loves playing guitar, as well as simply staring into space while listening to music.